THE CALYPSO CAPER

Also by Robert Dietrich

The Steve Bentley Thrillers

Murder on the Rocks
End of a Stripper
The House on Q Street
Mistress to Murder
Murder on Her Mind
Angel Eyes
Curtains for a Lover
Calypso Caper
Curtains for a Lover
My Body
Guilty Knowledge

THE CALYPSO CAPER

ROBERT DIETRICH

CUTTING EDGE

ISBN-13: 978-1-952138-34-8

Published by
Cutting Edge Publishing
PO Box 8212
Calabasas, CA 91372
www.cuttingedgebooks.com

CHAPTER ONE

The morning I flew over from San Juan to St. Thomas they found the naked body of Victor Polo floating off the Frenchtown docks, stabbed in the heart. An old Cha-Cha fisherman looped a line around one ankle, towed it in, and they carried it to a table in the Normandie Bar wondering who the goateed stiff was. Then an old Negro who had worked around Polo's Casino when it was still a gambling joint drifted in for a glass of warm gin and made him. A Cruzan guitarist collared a couple of steel band drummers and they coined a Calypso chant out of it on the spot. By noon all Charlotte Amalie knew the tune and the words.

But nobody knew why Victor Polo the gambler had come back to St. Thomas—or why he had been killed. And not many people cared. Only the Virgin Islands Police. And the murderer.

From the air that morning St. Thomas looked like a green jewel in a warm tourmaline sea. Against its bone white sand the lazy Caribbean rollers were wisps of cotton, and as the plane dropped lower I could see the spine of mountains topped by Signal Hill, the rusty tracery of dirt roads cut through heavy jungle, and the pink and white buildings of Charlotte Amalie sprawling to the west of the asphalt landing strip.

During the War the sheet-tin airport building had been a patrol plane hangar and it was as hot as a kiln inside. Once my bags were unloaded from the plane a straw-hatted boy carried them out and dropped them by a flaked sign that read: *Big John's Taxi Service.*

I tipped him and he drifted away with less noise than a heat wave. From the palm shadows a man detached himself and strolled toward me. He was a big man, black as anthracite, and his shoulders spread the width of a butcher's block. He wore a short-sleeved sport shirt and faded chinos and he looked cooler than a chocolate soda. "You Mistah Bentley?" he asked in a voice like a hoarse tuba.

"The same."

"Mistah Sonny Tyner called me to take you up to his place. I'm Big John." He stuck out a hand as big as a picnic ham and crushed my fingers cruelly. Pulling away what was left of my hand, I began massaging blood back into my knuckles. "Thanks for the welcome but I've been doing poorly lately. We'll shake again maybe when I get my strength back."

He grinned and his teeth were as white as ivory dice. Bending over, he picked up my bags and carried them toward a taxi as easily as a crane lifts a cardboard box. I followed, nursing my right hand, and got into the rear seat. He slid behind the wheel, slammed the rusty door shut and stamped on the starter. The motor exploded like a broken pony engine and the old car bounced over gravelly ruts until we were on Harwood Highway.

The road to Charlotte Amalie led past tottering Negro shacks with junkpile yards guarded by fierce and scrawny chickens. There was boiled wash on the lines and the scent of frying fish drifted through the heavy noonday heat.

Without turning, Big John called, "You come heah before?"

"Five years ago."

"Thought I remembered you. Nevah fo'get a face. You Mistah Tyner's lawyuh?"

"His tax man. I'm what they call a certified public accountant. Tax consultant. Figures and such."

His head half-turned. "A money-mon. I likes the money-mons."

"I only work with it."

"Mistah Tyner got it."

"He sure does. How's business been at The Lodge?"

"Good business in season. No business now. Too hot." He spat out of the window. "Too dom hot, mon."

I loosened my tie and mopped sweat from my throat. Off to the left, topping a low peak, rose a big white hotel. New since my last trip to the Virgins. It could have been air-lifted intact from Miami Beach and it looked air-conditioned. I wondered if Sonny had added air-conditioning to The Lodge. Probably not. Sonny was a millionaire who liked to think of himself as adventurous and hardy. I wondered why he had sent Big John to meet me instead of coming himself.

"Where's Mr. Tyner?" I asked. "Saint Croix?"

"No. He ovah Frenchtown. Foun' the body of Mistah Victah Polo in the watah this mo'nin'." He began chanting in shambling Calypso rhythm:

> Mistah Victah Polo was a Big Time Mon.
> He gamble for money wherevah he con.
> Win lotta money, then lose it, too.
> Mistah Victah Polo—he all through.

"You don't say," I said. "I remember the Casino when Polo ran it as a gambling joint. Until the Feds closed in. What happened to him?"

"Got clean away," Big John husked. "Nobody evah saw him again. Not until this mo'nin'. Maybe Mista Polo was bettah off at someplace else."

"Looks like."

He gestured with his right hand. "Road to Frenchtown. We could drop by the Normandie Bar and maybe nibble a couple. If you's hot an' thirsty, that is."

"I'm both," I said, "but we better keep going. If we stop I'm liable to melt down in a puddle like Black Sambo's tigers."

He chuckled and bore down on the accelerator. The old relic groaned and leaped ahead but the artificial breeze was worth the extra abuse.

We were passing the old French cemetery with its peeling whitewashed tombs and gnarled dead trees. Rusted iron fencing leaned crazily, half overgrown by thick spear grass. Unless someone could do better by him the late Victor Polo would be buried there. End of a gambling man.

At the edge of town we turned over and took the waterfront promenade where old Tortola Island luggers were unloading building material and contraband. Dirty canvas awnings draped over the booms gave shade to the drowsing crews. Off to the left a metal sign with an arrow pointed to a cool-looking building that faced the waterfront. The sign said: *Dominic's. Reba Royce and Her Bamboushay Calypsos Nightly from Nine O'Clock.* Bamboushay was Calypso for having yourself a big fat time.

Big John turned in past the courthouse and post office and the old car snarled up a steep hill lined with flaming bougainvillea and flamboyant trees heavy with foot-long seed pods. On Kongens Gade the tall balconied face of Government House looked as though it had been transplanted from the Vieux Carré, and beyond it hung a white wooden sign with blue letters: *The Lodge. Allegra & Vernon Tyner.*

The taxi stopped and I got out, fanning myself gently. Big John lifted out my bags and started carrying them up the steep stone steps. I followed, hoping a glass of icy beer would be waiting at the top.

The steep hillside was a tropical garden thick with century plants, hibiscus, bougainvillea and flowering oleander bushes.

Above it a shaded veranda with white post railings looked out over the harbor. As I reached it I saw Allegra sitting on a hassock beside a lean, gray-haired man in shorts and a spiked Guard's mustache. When she saw me she called, "*Steve!* Welcome back, stranger."

The man turned and glared at me. He was good at it. It could have been a full-time hobby. I turned to pay Big John but he had disappeared down the stairway. I figured he would bill The Lodge later.

Allegra Tyner came over to me, took my hand and kissed my cheek lightly. "Hello, paleface," she said. "Sonny'll be back any minute. He's down in Frenchtown. A man was—"

"I know," I said. "Victor Polo. I even heard the song. Kind of grisly even on such a sunny day."

She nodded thoughtfully, brightened and said, "Steve, this is Simon Hargrave. Simon, Steve Bentley from Washington. Our financial genius."

Hargrave unwound enough to shake hands with me. He had dark deep-set eyes and he looked decidedly fit for a man in his mid-fifties. He said grumpily, "Now you're here we can move ahead with the Coco Isle project. It's been stalemated while we waited for you."

"Steve has other clients," Allegra said. "Anyway, we're glad he's here. Steve, we're having banana daiquiris. Have one?"

"Sounds a mite cloying. I'll settle for some frosty lager."

Nodding, she clapped her hands and after a while a bare-footed Negro girl came out of the house and took my order. When she had gone away Allegra said, "Not a guest in the house except you, Steve, so we're putting you in the honeymoon suite upstairs. If you like it well enough maybe someday you'll bring along a bride."

"That's in the hands of the gods," I said, pulling off my wet tie, and sat down in a hammock. The harbor water was as calm as a silver mirror. A white-sailed lugger was drifting toward the

West Indies Docks. Beyond lay Hassel Island, one steep hill a water catchment faced with white concrete. A Volkswagen put-putted past. A gull sailed lazily through the sky and the sun on the roof made the porch hot enough for a coking oven. I undid my shirt buttons and pulled off my shirt. Hargrave harrumphed.

I said, "I'll slip into the tropical rig later."

The girl came back with a sweating bottle of Heineken's and a tall cone-shaped glass. Ignoring the glass, I tilted the bottle and let health and strength slide down my gullet. Puerto Rico's rain forest heat had used up most of my energy. I needed it back and the sooner the better.

Allegra had gone back to her seat beside Simon Hargrave. I didn't know how complicated putting together the Coco Isle development corporation would be but I had an idea the work wouldn't be facilitated by Hargrave. All I knew about him was that he had Chicago packing-house money and had settled in the Virgins after the War. Now Sonny Tyner, Hargrave and a Mrs. Vane Drury had secured a hundred-year lease on Coco Isle, off the north side of St. Thomas, and proposed to sell beach properties and put up a luxury hotel for tourists. Under Virgin Island law their corporation would be tax-exempt for ten years. An attractive investment for people with a lot of taxable income. Five years ago I had helped Sonny establish The Lodge under the same tax exemption and now he was asking for more. So I was combining business with a long-postponed vacation.

Hargrave finished his drink and stood up. "I'll be going," he announced. "Glad you're here, Bentley."

"Glad to be here, Hargrave," I said and enjoyed his scowl. I was a fetch-and-carry boy, not one of the landed gentry, and I would do well to remember my place. He clomped across the flooring and went down the steep stairway, his tall figure receding like the mast of a hull-down ship. "Nice guy," I said. "You need money that bad?"

Allegra shrugged. "He takes knowing, Steve. Simon's worse than the Cha-Chas when it comes to being suspicious of strangers. He's a friend of Sonny's. He brought him into the deal."

"What about Mrs. Drury?"

"She had the original option on Coco Isle but not enough capital to swing the financing. She and Hargrave are old friends—through her late husband. Vane's one of our Island characters. Wait'll you meet her."

"If she's anything like Hargrave I can wait indefinitely."

"Don't be ungenerous, Steve. More beer?"

"You might call for several," I said. "To save footwork."

When she had done same, she moved over near me and said, "Just don't ever mention Ralph Dominic to Mrs. Drury."

"The thought never occurred to me. But why not?"

"Dominic married her daughter, Sybil. The last time you were here she was just a spindly kid but she turned into an Island beauty."

"Same Dominic who runs the waterfront night club?"

She nodded. "He was the partner of Victor Polo, the man who was—"

"Yeah," I said sourly. "Mistah Polo was a Big Time Mon, but he's had it. So what about Dominic and Sybil?"

"He was a man of the world, a gambler and probably a crook, with enough magnetism to attract women like flies. Neither handsome nor pleasant. Well, Dominic got tired of playing house with Sybil—couldn't stand her wide-eyed adoration, I guess—and went back to his own ways if he ever stopped them. They're separated now—maybe even divorced—I haven't kept track. Anyway, Sybil still adores him, hangs around the bar at his place, drinking and keeping track of his latest doxies. All this infuriates Mrs. Vane Drury, who didn't raise her daughter to be a bartender's cast-off bride."

"Sort of messy," I murmured.

"Particularly here where you can't avoid seeing the same people every day. One of the curses of Island life."

"Tell me your troubles. Make me all misty-eyed over the general suffering in Saint Thomas."

Allegra smiled, straightened the front of her blouse and stood up. "Here's Sonny now."

He came plodding up the long stairway, a well-built man in his early forties with a lean face and falcon eyes. He was wearing a white polo shirt, long white shorts and black laceless loafers. His skin was the color of burnished bronze and the sun highlighted his graying hair.

He had reached the porch before he noticed me. His serious look gave way to a smile and he came over quickly and we shook hands. After pleasantries he called for a whisky and sat down near Allegra. Then he sucked a deep breath and said, "Sort of shook me seeing old Victor stretched out on two barroom tables. Indecent, somehow. And the goatee added to the grisly effect." He picked up his whisky glass, rattled the ice and gulped it. "Victor wasn't my favorite Thomian, but I never heard of his hurting anyone and he ran straight tables."

"Oh?" Allegra said archly. "Then all those expensive nights at the Casino you were just plain unlucky. I'd always thought of Victor as a modern highwayman and now you tell me he was as honest as a British banker. Or possibly the sight of his waterlogged corpse touched you unbearably."

"It gave me the chills," Sonny said moodily. "And seeing how much he'd aged in five years. God knows where he went, what he'd been doing."

"Or why he came back." Allegra got up, went over to the bamboo bar and I heard the whir of a blender liquefying another banana.

"Watch the calories," Sonny called.

"Calories aren't the only thing I'm watching these days, my love."

Sonny turned around, glowering. "She's got the warped notion I've got the hots for a mulata dancer down at Dominic's."

"Reba Royce and her Calypso funmakers?" I asked.

Allegra turned off the blender and gave a brittle laugh. "What sharp eyes you have," she purred. "Half an hour in Saint Thomas and Steve Bentley knows our latest scandal."

"Drop it," Sonny snapped. "She's Dominic's woman."

"His and anyone else's." Allegra came toward us, a banana daiquiri in her hand. "Anyone with pants and a ten-dollar bill. But that shouldn't trouble you, darling, you've developed such an itch for Sybil. Or is it that you just can't make up your mind which itch to favor?"

Sonny gave me a pained look, spread his hands helplessly and tossed off the rest of his drink. Then he got up and walked wordlessly to the bar. A small green parrot detached itself from the overhang and walked down a pillar to the floor. It came toward our table with ludicrously precise steps, climbed up one leg and began helping itself to the salted Brazil nuts. Having nothing to add to the conversation, I watched it feed gluttonously. Brazil nuts at two bucks a pound. The Tyner parrot. I opened another bottle of beer and wondered if I would fare as well.

Allegra was smoking nervously. After a while Sonny came back with a fresh drink. He sat near me and said, "Sorry about the outbreak of family tensions, Steve. Island living. What we probably need is a long vacation—from each other."

"How right you are, my love," Allegra murmured. "How soon can you leave?"

Sonny flushed. Without looking around at his wife, he said, "Just possibly you might be more comfortable somewhere else, Steve. Under the circumstances you're hardly under any obligation to stay here."

"Sorry, everybody," Allegra said, "I'll sheathe my claws for the day. I'm not always like this, Steve. Only when I get to thinking how rotten life can be."

Sonny turned and stared at her for a long time. The look on his face gave me the first chill I had felt since last winter. When he turned back to me he said, "I've got all the Coco Isle books and papers in my office. If the deal comes off it will involve close to four million dollars—land around here sells now for about five thousand an acre. Victor Polo's coming back just at this time could be only coincidence, but he had a long and sensitive nose where money was concerned. Ever since I heard he'd been killed I've been wondering if he didn't come back to a slice himself a piece of the Coco Isle cake—without an invitation."

CHAPTER TWO

The beach at Sapphire Bay turned out to be a wide scallop of ash-white sand with a cluster of cabanas, a barbecue grill and a flat-roofed open bar where they sold hot dogs and hamburgers at half a buck a bite. In mid-afternoon it was nearly deserted: a few kids with flippers and snorkels whose mothers guzzled iced rum in the shade, and a brace of ancient gorgons whose skins looked two sizes too large. Three lushly curved Thomian juveniles lay on a beach mat, giggling and taking turns rubbing sun oil on each others' limbs. Two fairies from Philadelphia held hands in the shade of a low palm tree. The air was still, the water warm and as clear as polished glass. Hull-down on the horizon a white racing yawl with a balloon spinnaker was making for St. Thomas, tacking methodically in search of a steady breeze. A boat over from St. Croix or up from the Antilles chain. As I watched it I envied the skipper and the crew.

An hour's sun seemed ample for the first day, so I took a fresh-water shower, squeezed into my rented Volkswagen and buzzed back around the coast road to town.

Fort Christian, the old Danish colonial stronghold, was a shadowed bulk of pink plaster as I drove around it and steered down to the waterfront where a big yawl was making fast to the pier. Braking, I stopped to admire its clean racing lines, sparkling paint and bright brasswork. Over fifty feet long, it was a yachtsman's dream.

As the stern swung close to the pier a figure came up out of the cabin, a bag in each hand, and leaped lightly ashore. The bags were white cowhide and matched. They looked expensive. The girl who was carrying them looked expensive, too. In the sunlight her hair was red gold. Knee-length white poplins clung to her tapering thighs and a tight green-silk blouse seemed barely a match for her high, firm breasts. Her skin was milky caramel and her sultry lips were toned the color of pink icing. She was walking quickly away from the boat, chin held haughtily high, her chest heaving. I got the idea that if she never saw the yawl again it would be entirely too soon.

Letting the Volks ease forward, I stopped across her path and looked up. "Taxi?" I asked cheerfully.

She stopped abruptly, gnawed her lip and lowered her bags. "No…no, thanks."

"Too hot to walk," I urged. "Ride now, pay later."

"E for Effort, but no sale, little man."

"Outside the midget car I'm normal size," I complained. "Anyway, this isn't really a taxi. So name it and we're there."

She picked up one bag, chewed her lip again and shook her head. The strawberry tresses spun out like a crimson fan and she said, "You picked the wrong moment, stranger. This is my day for hating men." Lifting one thigh, she balanced the bag awkwardly on it and opened the top. Sunlight glinted on metal. Blue metal. Gun steel. Suddenly I was staring into the muzzle of a small automatic pistol.

"Easy there," I croaked. "No offense, ma'am."

She laughed a short nervous laugh. "Don't think I can't use it."

"I wouldn't argue for the world."

"You're blocking my path."

I let the Volks into gear and pulled ahead, angling over toward the pier. The redhead was tucking her pistol back into her bag. Closing the bag, she picked both up and continued on across the pier to the edge of the waterfront. I mopped sweat from my face, shrugged and idled the Volks over toward where two Negro crewmen were adjusting gunwale fenders and snubbing the lines around pier bitts. A man in a yachting cap, white ducks and sneakers sprawled in the cockpit, sucking on a bottle of beer. I poked my head out of the window and called, "Charter boat?"

"Yeah."

"Been out long?"

He spat over the side, wiped his lips on his arm and said, "Too damn long. Trinidad and back. Her husband jumped ship at Martinique last week. And him owing for the whole charter." He adjusted the bottle to his lips, leaned back and drained it. The Negroes were sitting on the pier, dangling their feet over the edge. Both of them wore high-crowned straw Cha-Cha hats broken at the edges. The bottle sailed through the air and plopped into the water. The skipper stood up and stretched. "Two thousand skins," he said disgustedly. "Who the hell can you trust these days?"

The Negroes looked at each other and rolled their eyes worriedly. One of them said, "Cap'n Andersen, you ain' forgettin' us?"

The captain put his hands on his hips and stared at them. "I never yet forgot you. Beat it."

The Negroes got up and shuffled away, ragged pants and bare feet. The captain stared after them, shook his head and went down into the cabin. Turning, I looked back toward town but the red-haired girl had disappeared. I put my foot on the accelerator, pushed the car into gear and scuttled across the waterfront and up the hill to The Lodge.

It was too hot to sleep. Too hot and too much light. Caked paint had glued the louvered shutters open. There were flies in the room. They lit on my sweating body and buzzed away. A lot of flies and no breeze. After a while I dozed. When I pulled myself off the bed I felt as if I had been battling a laundromat. I needed a shave but my stubble was slick with sweat. Pushing the shutters open I saw a palm branch stir. Evening breeze—if you could call it that. From the porch below I could hear the whir of the blender beating another banana to death. The local diet was sensational: mashed fruit and rum. I peered at myself in the wash basin mirror and tried to remember if the redhead had violet eyes or if the whole thing had been a mirage. Heat like that could do anything. I slumped onto the bed again, made myself breathe deeply and when I had enough strength I pulled on some shorts, walking socks, sandals and a short-sleeved shirt. Except for the lobster tint I could pass for a native. Well, the Tyners had warned me ....

The porch was ten degrees cooler and the Tyners were doing some light drinking. I waved aside a banana daiquiri and elected rum Coke. Sonny looked morose and Allegra was maintaining a hostile silence. The atmosphere was twice as cheerful as Death Row.

Allegra said, "That's quite a burn, Steve."

"It'll do for a start."

Sonny said, "Man has two natural enemies in the tropics: sun and drink."

"And women," Allegra added.

"I nearly forgot. Most of all women. The deadliest."

I sucked on my drink and said nothing.

Allegra lighted a cigarette, let smoke drift across the table and looked up at the pet parrot. "Rip Andersen's back," she remarked. "The girl came with him—the friend didn't."

"What girl, what friend?"

"Kelly Martin—as if you didn't know." She glanced at me. "Quite a dish, Steve. If you like the type."

"I do," I said. "I like the type better than almost any other."

Allegra laughed condescendingly. "You haven't even seen her—unless you remember some of her pictures. She was Tarzan's bride or something equally challenging, I believe."

"The hell she was," Sonny said. "She had several good parts. Then her option expired."

"I wonder why," his wife cooed.

"That's Hollywood. One day a contract, the next day Zilch."

"I might have known you'd have all the details, darling. If there were any gaps before you can fill them in at leisure. She's back now and without that annoying friend of hers."

"Her husband," Sonny said.

Allegra laughed coolly, got up and walked into the house. "Jesus Christ," Sonny said bitterly. "When I was courting my wife I thought her serpent's tongue was a houseful of laughs. Now it's just a serpent's tongue. You're a bachelor, Steve. Stay that way. This is the voice of experience speaking."

"I haven't had a good offer in weeks."

"Just as well. Sometimes I feel boxed in on all sides. Living down here's done it. If I were smart we'd chuck the whole damn thing and charge off to Europe for a year, get our balance back." He tilted his glass and stared off beyond the railing at the houses rising steeply away from the harbor. Washed in faded colors they looked like a toy village that had stood too long in the sun.

I said, "I saw the Martin girl leave the yawl. What's her problem?"

He turned back to me and shrugged. "Money, probably. Fellow she came here with was a big spender but he didn't look her type—more the Madison Ad-man style. One of our gossips hinted Kelly was trying to crash the modeling business by being nice to the boss, but hell, it could be just another Island slander. Stay here long enough and you'll be able to catalogue libel by size, shape and color. Hargrave took a shine to her but she was under heavy escort at the time. If she's back and on the beach Simon may get another chance."

"Hargrave doesn't look her type, either."

"To a girl like her money means a lot."

"It means a lot to anyone who hasn't taken priestly vows."

"I suppose so," he said moodily. "Tomorrow we can get down to business. What we need tonight are a few laughs. With or without my wife's company. Roger?"

I nodded and finished my drink. "Anyone ever eat around here?"

"Now and then. Down here you get away from regular hours and balanced meals. Any routine loses its importance. Your focus changes, you drink too much, do too little, and everything's the same. Right now I don't even know why I got into this Coco Isle scheme. Boredom, I guess. And an escape from my vixen wife."

A maid came out from the house and took my order for roast beef sandwiches and salad. Keep it light with an accent on the proteins. Lighting a cigarette, I said, "Any reason I can't go over the papers now? I left Washington only last night and I'm still in the habit of working an hour or so a day."

Sonny shrugged. "Sure, I'm the slothful one. I'd back out of this if it weren't for Simon. He's kind of a bastard but I like him. No, I admire him and that's not the same thing."

"Why?"

He looked down at his empty glass. "Simon's shrewd and he's hard and he's hell with the women. Qualities I don't mind saying I envy. At his age they seem outstanding." He looked up with a rueful smile. "Now that I've said it, it doesn't seem very substantial."

I shook my head.

"I said you lose focus down here." He got up, went into the house and came back with an armful of manila folders and account ledgers. "It's all here," he said as he dumped it on the table in front of me. "Have yourself a big time with it. I'm going to flake out for an hour or so. We might even make this an all-nighter."

He went away. I got up and made another rum Coke. By then the maid had brought my order and while I munched my sandwiches I began going over the incorporation papers. The preliminary work had been done by a Charlotte Amalie lawyer well-versed in tax angles, and what was left to me was preparing an amortization program that tied into the Virgin Islands special tax exemptions. It was a job that could take a week or a month, depending on how long I wanted it to last and how quickly the principals reached agreement on my proposals. The trouble was the setting was wrong for serious work: palm trees and bird-of-paradise flowers, tropical birds and wet heat and a crystal sea around me. Grand for a vacation but I could see why things were done slowly in the tropics. If at all. Getting out a legal-size writing pad, I leafed through the papers and began making notes.

When light was nearly gone the maid shuffled out and turned on electrified hurricane lamps with copper bases. I stretched my arms, blinked and gathered my work together. Then I climbed up to my room, shaved, took a shower and got into dry clothes. When I came down again Sonny was waiting for me, a drink in his hand.

"We might start out at The Gate," he said. "It's no novelty for me but maybe you like steel bands."

We walked down the steps together, squeezed into my Volks and Sonny guided me through narrow lanes bordered by shuttered shop fronts and high arched doorways. Gift shoppes and liquor stores and apothecaries, tearoom-style restaurants and tropical haberdasheries. And overhead a deep violet sky.

The Gate looked like something out of a cleaned-up Casbah. Long low seats and tables and a mixed crowd of colored and whites dancing to the heavy din of an eight-piece steel drum band. The drummers were all Negroes with oil-drum instruments painted garish red and yellow. They chanted and swayed and high school kids lining the rear stairway peered down at the moving crowd under the arched pillars. Anyone not dancing was drinking. Sonny shook hands with a lot of people, waved at others and a waiter found us a lounge in the corner and threaded his way back to the bar with our order for tall rum drinks.

Most of the females were dancing barefoot to the sinuous hip-rolling rhythm. The men wore shorts and sandals and short-sleeved sport shirts. Lighting a cigarette, I listened to the band start "Congo Train." Dancers traded partners and began again. Hot work, but pleasant. Sonny said, "This gets pretty damn old after five years, Steve. People only come here to see who's dancing with who."

Our drinks arrived and I removed the straws for better access. Sweat was girdling my neck. The place had everything except ventilation. A thick belt of smoke clung solidly to the ceiling. Sonny guzzled his rum and stared heavily at the crowd. A few more drinks and he would either perk up or pass out. We stayed until the band left for intermission and then we went out on the street where it was easily fifteen degrees cooler. Sonny said, "We'll try Dominic's. Simon'll probably be there." He glanced at his watch and we started down an alley toward the waterfront, keeping a good margin away from the open sewer. Past shops whose stolid iron-plated doors were relics of days when waterfront buildings were warehouses and the town was the biggest slave-market in the world. Then the lights bordering the waterfront spread out along the promenade, and a car idled past the docked luggers with kerosene lanterns swaying gently from their booms. I thought I could see Big John's taxi parked near the water but it was too far away and the light was too bad to be sure.

There was a whisper of a breeze stirring the leaves of pigmy palms as we turned into the yard of Dominic's. The notes of a piano drifted through the air along with the quiet sound of voices and the tinkle of ice in tall glasses.

Inside, low lights and a small band platform with a spidery pianist bending over the keys. Tables the size of snare drums and couples holding hands in the dimness. A long bamboo bar on the porch, two Negro bartenders and a man leaning back against the liquor shelf near the cash register. A medium-sized man with slick black hair and an olive skin. He had eyes that popped slightly and he was smoking a thick cigar. His face was plump but not fat and his arms and shoulders looked powerful. His fingers withdrew the cigar and his eyes gazed into the dimness. There was a slight sneer on his lips.

On the bar stools half a dozen people, mixed as to sex, but united in common pursuit of the demon rum. I climbed onto a stool and Sonny mounted one beside me. He put his elbows on the bar and spoke to the man with the cigar. "Hello, Dominic," he said in an odd voice. "Two rum sours."

Dominic's face turned slightly until he was looking at Sonny. "Hello, Tyner," he said unpleasantly. "Slumming tonight, or catting after Reba again?"

Sonny half rose from his seat but I pulled him back.

Dominic regarded him stolidly, drew back his lips and spat on the floor. Then he turned and walked out on the porch. I watched him go and, as my head turned, I realized that a girl sitting on the stool beside me was regarding me with an amused smile. Her lips were a little loose, as though she had been drinking for quite a while, and when she spoke her words were slightly slurred. "Hello, cabbie," she said. "How you do get around." Even in the dimness I could see her violet eyes.

"It's the miracle of modern transportation," I said. "Footwork gets you almost anywhere—Mrs. Martin."

Her lips set firmly and she reached for her glass and tilted it. When she put it down she kept on staring at it and said, "You've made inquiries, haven't you?"

"It isn't every day a pistol-packin' redhead gets the drop on me. Then, too, just by being around a town like this someone like you creates her own legend. Or hadn't that occurred to you?"

Her face turned slowly and she said, "Cigarette, please."

I gave her one and lighted it. "Thanks," she said. "It's good to be back in civilization again. If you can call it that."

"That would depend on where you've been. And how long."

She smiled wryly. "There's truth in that. What's your name?"

I told her.

"A nice name," she murmured. "Are you a nice guy as well?"

"There's mixed opinion on that. My friends speak well of me, my enemies evil."

"You have enemies?"

"Doesn't everyone?"

She blew smoke across the bar and looked down at her cigarette. "Sometimes the biggest enemy is right inside you."

"If you let it stay."

She nodded. "There's that."

The bartender placed drinks in front of Sonny and me. I lifted my glass and said, "Luck, Kelly."

She lifted her glass wordlessly and from the darkness beyond the bandstand a woman walked toward the bar. Her skin was the color of light cocoa and she moved with feral pride, hips rolling slightly, breasts swaying tautly against their crossed bandana halter. She was erect and relaxed in a way common to all Negresses and hardly any white women. Her shoulder-length black hair was nearly straight, her nostrils only slightly flattened. Her full lips held a sardonic curve. She was wearing a vivid flower-patterned skirt that accented the naked skin below her halter. As she passed behind me her sandals made little hushed sounds on the floorboards. I turned and saw that Sonny was staring at her. She was almost past him when he reached out and caught her wrist. "Don't try to brush me off, Reba," he whispered hoarsely. "Not after all—"

Dominic had materialized from the shadows. "Get your hands off her," he snapped.

Sonny slid down from his stool and Reba's arm dropped free. She jerked it against her flesh and felt her wrist tenderly.

"You her keeper?" Sonny sneered.

"She works here. Nobody paws the help."

"Nobody except Dominic."

Reba's eyes glistened like opals. She liked it. She liked it a lot.

I put my hand on Sonny's shoulder. "Relax."

He shook me off and made a wild swing at Dominic.

The punch hit just below the other man's ribs. Breath escaped him in a long sigh, his lips twisted and then he hit Sonny in the belly. Sonny doubled over and Dominic's other fist connected with his temple. Sonny crashed back against the bar, arms windmilling, but his eyes were glassy. I caught him under the shoulders and held him like a sack of stones.

Behind me Kelly murmured, "Such lively friends you have."

Dominic flexed his knuckles, rasped, "Out, Reba," and stalked back into the shadows of the porch. I felt Sonny's knees stiffen and take some of his weight. Then he struggled upright, glaring wildly at the emptiness ahead of him.

I said, "Lesson number one: never start something you can't finish."

Kelly laughed tightly.

Sonny snarled, "I'll kill the bastard!"

"Over a mulata?" I shook my head. "The press would love it. Not to mention your kids' prep school companions. Let it go. Get hold of yourself and do a little sober thinking."

As he listened the insanity flickered out of his eyes. He wiped his mouth and one hand reached up and touched his temple. "Jesus," he said huskily, "I must be going crazy." He shook his head dazedly, blinked and made a vague gesture. "I'm going back. Got to talk to Allegra...explain..." He looked at me vacantly. "You stay here." Then he turned and went unsteadily across the floor and out into the night.

All conversation had stopped but now the murmurs began and grew. I swung around and picked up my drink. Kelly was watching me with speculative eyes. "Well," she said, "just where does that leave us?"

CHAPTER THREE

"It leaves us with a couple of unfinished drinks and the rest of the night to kill."

She nodded, lifted her glass and sipped slowly. Her eyebrows were wide and arching and her triangular face was charged with feline provocativeness. Putting down her glass, she looked across at the stepped rows of liquor bottles and said, "Gamy little scene, wasn't it? I haven't had a man throw a punch in my behalf in so long I can't remember what it feels like."

"It feels pretty good," I said, "and I imagine you've enjoyed your share of personal triumphs. Now, before we stray deeper into other things, suppose you define your status."

"Does it make a difference?"

"It could."

She shrugged, drew in on her cigarette and let smoke glide slowly from her nostrils. "We were going to be married," she said in a remote voice. "Somewhere during the cruise the idea drifted away. Don't ask me why. Or even how it came up in the first place." Her head turned slowly and her eyes were smoky and deep. "That makes me a fallen woman, doesn't it?"

"Not alone it doesn't."

Her lips tightened, then relaxed. "I was born plain Jean O'Houlihan. When I was seventeen Paramount gave me a contract. If you've ever seen me in pictures I'd rather you forgot it. You know the tired old Hollywood story, I'm sure. Well, most of it happened to me. So if you were shocked that I'd go off for a month with a man not my husband that might help to explain why." She stubbed out her cigarette. "I don't even know why I'm talking to you. When I got off the boat I told you this was my day for hating men."

"The day ends at midnight."

She smiled slightly. "But I won't change into anything different, like Cinderella."

"Well, I might. I've been known to turn into a rat. Even before midnight."

She laughed. "I guess you can spot a damsel in distress when you see one."

"What happened to the picture business?"

"*Me* and the picture business?"

"I didn't say that."

"Well, the smart money always said they'd eventually run pictures into the ground—and they did. Have you been out to Hollywood lately?"

"No."

"It looks like Oil City, Oklahoma. Derricks and oil pumps where executive offices used to be. But for the oil royalties there wouldn't be half so many pictures produced."

"Is that the whole story?"

She shrugged. "Are you up to hearing the details?"

"If you're up to telling them."

"My producer was a nice guy. Married to a one-time Miss America, two boys at Black-Foxe and a daughter at Mills. A nice guy. The last time option time came around he made a simple request." She turned away from me. "I don't know why I should have been so surprised. Lou didn't want very much—he didn't even want to go to bed with me. It all could have been taken care of right there in his office. A simple request, harmful to no one. I was to take off my clothes...."

"Was that all?"

"That was to be only the beginning. Have you read Kraft-Ebbing lately?"

"Not since I was twelve."

"Well, try to imagine the weird details. Anyway, I pulled the Outraged Hannah bit and flounced out. Now that I think back on it, I wonder if I handled the scene as artfully as I might have."

"Well—you left with your principles preserved."

"As if they can warm a girl on a cold night."

"What are you going to do now?"

Her head tilted slightly. "I wish I knew. I need a little time to think things through. I've hit low points before but this is bottom for me. Go back to New York eventually, I suppose, but I don't want to think about it now. Not just yet." She pushed her empty glass across the bar. The bartender took it away and mixed another drink. Then he did the same for me and leaned forward confidentially. "Who's payin' fo' Mistah Tyner's drink?"

"I am," I said. "Don't let it worry you."

Kelly said, "Dominic gave me a room here. Said I could stay as long as I liked. It's not much, but then it's free."

"How did you know him?"

"I only met him today. A few months ago a friend of his gave me his name. A man I met out in Vegas. He said he might see me here. He was a man doing a lot of gambling there."

"Successfully?"

"Probably not. I didn't particularly like him, but I remembered his name and today it did me some good. A bald man with a gray goatee."

"Victor Polo."

Her eyes widened. "How would you know that?"

"He did what he said he would. He came back to Saint Thomas. This morning they fished his body out of the water down in Frenchtown. With a knife wound through his heart."

In the darkness her face paled. "Dominic didn't tell me."

"Probably he didn't care. They were partners once in a gambling joint. Sometimes partnerships work out that way."

Her head had turned and she was looking out toward the porch where Dominic sat in the shadows facing the harbor. Picking up her glass, she drank quickly and put it down. Her chin tilted up and she breathed deeply. "Just like that. This becomes a more charming place than I suspected it was. Now I suppose my host will be under suspicion."

I shook out a cigarette for her and lighted it. She pushed back from the bar a little and looked up at the murky ceiling. "Are the police any good? Could they find a crashed plane on the main street?"

"Murder's a little different," I said. "The local cops have the advantage of knowing the scene, the people involved. When they need crime lab help there's a Bureau man drifting around in the background. He'll move in when he's asked, but not before."

Her nose wrinkled. "The FBI?"

"This is Federal territory. Not many crimes of violence but enough smuggling and such-like to keep them in practice."

"What about gambling?"

"It got organized during the War when this was a naval base—bored sailors on a tropical isle with loose cash in their trousers. In those days everyone winked at it, but when the patriotic glow wore off the bloodhounds snuffed it out. Exit Victor Polo."

She nodded thoughtfully. "What brings you here?"

I told her.

"Your life sounds steady and even-keeled. I think I envy you."

"Washington can be a lively town—after dark and behind shuttered windows."

"Babylon on the Potomac," she kidded.

The pianist was playing with closed eyes and an earnest, lost expression. He was no Joe Bushkin on the keys but for Charlotte Amalie he was probably tops. He modulated into "Black Coffee" and a man came from behind the bandstand, stepped up and slid behind the traps to add a little light brush work. The setting was becoming dreamily unreal. For the first time since touching down at the airport I was beginning to relax. I thought about Sonny's scrap with Dominic and found I didn't care about it one way or the other. Except for Allegra. A good way to get along in an insulated community was by minding your own business.

Kelly said, "A cruise ship's due in this week. I might take it back to New York. I can always model for the Montgomery Ward summer catalog. Spinster section."

"Riding yourself a little hard, aren't you?"

"Maybe I've got it coming."

A string bass made a trio on the bandstand. I drew her onto the dance floor, she dropped her sandals near the edge and we began to dance. She followed fluidly, effortlessly, eyes half closed, her chin against the side of my neck. The other couples were shadows around us. We danced for a long time, until the musicians left the stand and clustered around the end of the bar. We went back to our seats then, got some fresh drinks, and some Calypso musicians came from behind the bandstand with steel drums and bongos. They played swaying, plucking melodies, their faces like ebony statues. After that the steel drum men faded away, leaving two men with bongos who squatted on their haunches and struck a spattering metallic rhythm. A ceiling spot went on and out of the darkness ran a girl in a Calypso skirt with a red bandana around her hair. Reba Royce. Her skirt was divided in front, showing a red silk loincloth. She danced with jungle abandon, everything moving at once, her superbly muscled legs stabbing like lances at the floor, finishing finally to loud applause. By now all the tables were filled. Dominic sat on the porch railing, arms folded, watching her with steely eyes.

The drummers began a slower, more sensuous rhythm and she dipped low in whirling strides that took her around the perimeter of the floor. A hand darted behind her back, freed one knot of the halter and whipped away the bandana, twirling it like a flame as she crouched and spun to the hypnotic rhythm. A sigh went around the dark room as her other hand freed the other bandana. The cloths in her hands were veils for a Herod. Her rib cage showed delicately through her smooth flesh. Her taut, half-moon breasts lifted sulkily with her arms and Kelly whispered, "God, what a magnificent body. I can't really blame your friend, Steve."

I licked my lips and wet my dry throat with cool rum. There was a night breeze, but inside the temperature had risen thirty degrees. Reba's teeth glinted like milky porcelain and her nostrils flared with the effort of her dance. Little drops of moisture showed in the hollow of her throat. The drums reached a wild climax, Reba spun to the floor, fell to her knees and lifted her arms. The drums hit a single sharp beat and the light cut out. She rose in the darkness and ran around the bandstand into the shadows. The applause was loud and prolonged. When it died away the three musicians climbed back on the bandstand and began to play "Basin Street." But it was anticlimax. After Reba's performance waltzing elephants would have been.

Dominic was behind the bar again, doing something with the cash register. Streaks of sweat showed through the back of his shirt. In through the entrance came two women, one tall and slim, the older one gray-haired and shapeless. They took seats at the bar and stared at Dominic's back. Finally the older one snapped, "Bartender, two ladies would like some service."

Dominic turned slowly and glanced at them. Then he turned back to what he had been doing. The tall girl put her hand on the other woman's arm. "Don't make a scene, mother," she said.

Her face was a long oval, dark hair parted at the crown and drawn behind in a bun. A girl in her early twenties with good bones and an astringent figure. Her mother glanced sideways at her and said sharply, "I will do exactly as I please, Sybil. So long as you insist on coming to this rat-infested bar, I will demand the service we are entitled to." Staring at Dominic's back she rasped, "Service, bartender. The best in this broken-down saloon."

Dominic looked around, then turned and faced her. "Hello, mother," he said insolently. "Get out of here and haul that calf-faced daughter of yours with you."

Mrs. Vane Drury rose apoplectically, searched for something to throw and subsided. Dominic sauntered over and said, "Sybil, why don't you stay the hell away from here?"

"I don't want to."

"That's an intelligent answer," Dominic sneered. "Where the hell's your pride?"

Mrs. Drury laughed bitterly. "She lost it when she married a pig like you."

Hollows formed in Dominic's round face. His eyes were slits. Against the bar his hands opened and closed. "I'm sick of you," he grated. "You old horror, you're enough to make a man vomit. Now get out!"

Sybil rose, lips tremulous. "Ralph—please. If we could only talk…"

"Talk? You had your say, baby. You and the old hag who suckled you. I thought I was marrying a woman—a flesh and blood woman. What I got was a skinny bag of bones."

"At least her skin was white," Mrs. Drury hissed. "That was Sybil's only fault. That and the fact that I was foresighted enough to keep her money in trust—where you couldn't get it."

The muscles of his face were jerking like hidden wires. He leaned closer and snarled, "Keep it up, Vane, and I'll kill you."

Mrs. Drury pushed herself away from the bar. "I'm sure you're capable of it. And of course you've had recent practice. Or haven't they officially accused you of murdering Victor Polo?"

Dominic looked like a hunted dog. His breath came in harsh spasms. Abruptly Mrs. Drury stepped down from her stool, took Sybil's arm and pulled her away. Together they walked rapidly toward the doorway. Sybil turned and gazed back longingly at Dominic, but he was pouring himself a drink. A stiff one. Wiping his arm across his mouth, he glanced around the bar and stalked back behind the bandstand.

I reached for a cigarette, lighted it and mopped my forehead. Kelly said, "A lovely scene, Steve. This is one way to learn about one's host. What a dreadful old gorgon that woman is."

"And she's my client," I said. "The thought alone calls for another drink."

We downed another pair and when it was out of the way I realized that my toes were getting numb. My vision was worsening, too. What I needed was a hike in the cool night air. I suggested it to Kelly.

When I had paid the score we went out of Dominic's arm in arm and strolled unsteadily toward the waterfront.

"I like the atmosphere at Dominic's," I murmured. "Homey and cordial, a place where everyone's welcome. Cheery as an Irish pub. It has everything except the dart board."

"But the clients bring their own knives. Do you think—possibly—that we've had just the slightest bit too much to drink?"

"After what we've witnessed I'd say we haven't had half enough. We could climb up to The Lodge except for the Tyner family problems that are being discussed there right now. The liquor stores are locked and barred, so that's out. What do you suggest?"

"We could take a long drive."

"That takes a car." Turning back, we trudged back past Dominic's and scaled the hill beyond The Gate where the Volks was parked. We got in, I started the engine, and the little car jounced around and headed west toward Frenchtown, then up the hill to an overlook.

Through the windshield we could see the lights of Charlotte Amalie glimmering like distant fireflies below us. The night wind blew her hair across her forehead. Opening the door, she got out and sat on the low stone wall. I found cigarettes and joined her. After a while she leaned over against me and put her head lightly against my shoulder. One fist pressed against her mouth, her body shuddered and quietly she began to sob.

I held her in my arms until the spasm had spent itself. Then she sat up, dabbed at her eyes with a handkerchief and said, "Thanks for not asking a lot of questions. Men are so much better at moments like that. Women feel they have to make comforting noises." She tucked away her handkerchief and her face turned toward me. "I've made a mess of my life and I realize it. Only there's nothing I can do about it now."

The moon was a silver crescent over the tip of the island. It looked close enough to touch. Drawing her against me, I kissed her lips. They were cool and passionless, the lips of a stranger in the night, as remote as icy stars. After a while I said, "Sorry, Kelly."

"No. It's just that it's been a bad day and a bad month before it. You'll be around a while, won't you?"

"Sure." I drew her to her feet and guided her back to the Volks. Then I started the engine, turned around and headed down the hill toward town.

It was a narrow road, bordered with tropical foliage, lush plants with giant leaves and a tracery of spiny fronds. The road angled sharply and began to level out.

Then at the seaward edge of the road I saw something that made me jam on the brakes. Kelly glanced at me in surprise, then she saw it, too, and breath caught in her throat. I pushed open the door and got out quickly.

Ahead, in the glare of the headlights, lay an arm, fingers arched like claws digging into the crushed coral border. Beyond the arm a head and a body. I heard Kelly's door open and close behind me.

Kneeling, I stared at the body of a dead woman. Two crossed bandanas made a halter for her crushed breasts. Another bandana bound her black hair and her face was a slice of horror.

Buried under her right shoulder blade was the black haft of a small knife. Blood glinted on her smooth brown skin. A thick tendril of blood hung from the corner of her contorted mouth. Where the third finger of her left hand had been there was only a bloody stump; the rest had been hacked away.

Footsteps behind me. Kelly. I turned to tell her to get back in the car but she had already seen all there was to see.

"It's—it's the dancer," she said huskily. "Reba. *Oh, God!*"

CHAPTER FOUR

While Kelly drove down to Fort Christian for the police I had stayed with Reba's body. Thorns had torn Reba's flesh and clothing as she had crawled through the underbrush like a wounded animal. Later, in the dim light of a room in old Fort Christian, we had told our story to three colored policemen, signed statements and were released. By then the grayness of false dawn was a broad arc on the horizon and both of us were icily sober.

Now, in the late morning, I walked down the staircase from my room to the veranda. Allegra and Simon Hargrave were there, and the Negro maid. They watched me silently as I crossed to a coffee table and sat down. To the maid I said, "Eggs, juice and coffee."

She sidled away toward the kitchen. I shook out a cigarette and lighted it. Allegra and Simon stared at me as though I were a ghost. I said, "Where's Sonny?"

It was Hargrave who spoke. His voice was deep and funereal. "Down at Fort Christian."

"Doing what?"

He and Allegra exchanged glances. "Explaining his movements of last night."

Allegra took a deep breath and pulled herself erect. "Steve, what time did he leave you?"

"Ten or so." I watched the pet parrot start to descend from its ceiling sanctuary. "He said he was coming back here."

Allegra bit her lip. Simon glanced at her. "All you have to say is that he returned here a little after ten."

I said, "I see. What time did Sonny really come home?"

"That's the crux of the problem," Hargrave said heavily. "No one knows. Not even Sonny. He'd had quite a bit to drink, he said, so when he got back he stumbled into one of the empty rooms and slept until the police came here at eight o'clock. I'm inclined to believe him, but whether the police will is another matter entirely."

Allegra said, "Why would he kill her? He had no reason to. None at all." Her voice rose until Hargrave gripped her arm. "Steady," he said. "It's helping Sonny we've got to concentrate on." He looked over at me. "You could help there, Bentley."

"How?"

"Sonny needs an alibi."

"The last time I saw him was around ten last night."

"Maybe you could improve on that."

"I was with a young lady. We've already made statements to the police."

"Couldn't you change them?"

"Not without making liars of two people."

Hargrave glared at me. "Compared to the spot Sonny's in that doesn't seem terribly important."

"Look," I said. "My morals are pretty flexible, but they balk at perjury and that's just what you're suggesting. Last night at Dominic's Sonny had a few drinks and he stopped Reba to talk to her. That doesn't mean he killed her. Even as circumstantial evidence it's featherweight, so let's stop the crepe-hanging. Maybe one of the servants heard him come in last night. Have you asked?"

"Yes," Allegra said tightly. "The maid said she heard him come back after midnight. That's what we were talking about just now." Her face was a frightened face, drawn and colorless. Since yesterday she had aged ten years.

Hargrave said, "I'll talk to the girl, persuade her to change her story. She'll have her price." His voice sounded cynically confident.

I said, "You're both jumping at conclusions—unless there's some facts I don't know about."

Allegra's hands became fists. Her knuckles were as white as scraped bone.

Hargrave cleared his throat. He eased forward and said quietly, "There were bloodstains on Sonny's clothing. There were fresh scabs on his knuckles. He said he'd fallen climbing the steps."

"They can analyze the stains for blood group and race. If it's his own blood it can be proven."

Tightly Allegra said, "What if it isn't, Steve?"

"That'll be the time to worry," I told her, and watched the maid come in with my breakfast tray. While she was serving me Hargrave went over to the bar and mixed two long drinks. No banana mush today, the drinking was straight and serious. When the maid went away Hargrave came over beside me and sat down. I tossed off my juice, added cream and sugar to my coffee and began working on my eggs. Hargrave watched for a while and then he said, "It seems to me you're taking all this pretty lightly."

I rinsed my mouth with coffee and put down the cup. "What would be your idea? Picket Fort Christian until they let Sonny go?"

Allegra said, "Please, Simon. Steve may be right and we're making too much of this."

Hargrave laughed unpleasantly. "Before Bentley came here you told me he was the Washington police department's little helper—an amateur detective of sorts. Well, I haven't seen any signs of it yet."

I opened my mouth to say something corrosive but Allegra spoke up. "Steve will do whatever he can, I'm sure."

I finished my coffee and toast. Hargrave drank moodily and the veranda was silent. The parrot climbed up on the table and took possession of the toast crusts. It stared at me with beady challenging eyes but I was in no mood for a fight. Lighting a cigarette, I eased back against the cushions and said, "From what I saw of Reba last night, there'll be men in her past. Ralph Dominic, for example. Probably more."

Allegra said, "It's not quite that simple, or detached, Steve. Sonny was infatuated with her. He bought a house for her up on Crown Mountain. He used to visit her there. I followed him once. I never went back."

It was starting to get me. In spite of the hot coffee my stomach was chilled. Hargrave was nodding.

Allegra said, "I thought it was all over between them. Now I'm wondering if it really was."

Hargrave said, "Everyone knew about it. I tried to talk to Sonny but he wouldn't listen."

I said, "Last night when he left me Sonny was on his way here to talk to Allegra. He wanted to explain, ask forgiveness. He wasn't in any murdering mood. That much I know."

Hargrave finished his drink and stood up. "Let's hope so. I'm going down to Fort Christian and see if there's anything I can do." He looked over at Allegra. "Try to relax. I'll call you later."

She nodded dumbly. Hargrave turned and went down the steps. The maid came in and took away my tray. Allegra looked after her with pleading eyes. When we were alone, I got up and went over to her. "This sort of shoots the business problems, doesn't it?"

"At least until Sonny's cleared."

"I saw Mrs. Drury last night. At her imperious best. And her daughter. From what I saw Sybil was never a match for Dominic. He's three-fourths iron and one-quarter olive oil. I got the idea he looked on Reba as personal property."

Allegra looked up at me. "I could believe *anything* about Dominic. Already everyone believes he killed Victor Polo."

"Gossip," I said. "Where's the proof?"

"People don't need proof down here. They've convicted Sonny already."

"Then we'll have to un-convict him," I told her cheerfully. "Meantime, the best thing you can do is stand by him."

She nodded. "And what will you do, Steve?"

"Me? I'll start looking around."

"Thank you," she said tremulously. "Could there be a connection between Polo's murder and Reba?"

"Of course. And there could be no connection at all. Sometimes murder comes in rashes. One killing can make another one necessary. Or someone who's been waiting to kill hears of a murder and decides the time is ripe, adding the element of confusion. What about the house on Crown Mountain?"

She got up, went over to a cabinet and brought back a paper place mat. On it was printed a map of St. Thomas. She made a pencil mark on it, folded the map and gave it to me. "What else, Steve?"

"Get your mind off it."

"I'll try."

The crimson bougainvillea flowers were alive with pollen-dusted bees as I walked down the steps to the parking area where I had left my Volks. The inside was so hot I had to open both doors and wait for the air to cool. Then I got inside and drove down the hill and over past the old native market. Donkeys were tethered near piles of fresh vegetables and hampers of lush flowers. Scrawny dogs and cats disputed gutter offal from the butcher's stalls. In a shaded doorway a little naked Negro child hummed himself a tuneless song.

Street shops were open for business. Scotch at three bucks a fifth, Madras shirts and dresses, Italian firearms, French perfumes, Irish linens, Swiss watches and all the other merchandise of a duty-free port. Even at cut rates it still took money to buy. Genteel, condescending, Island-born tradespeople to take your money and sneer at you for having it. Record shops blared too-loud Calypso records. Tourists in noisy sport shirts strolled along the streets, cameras in hand, chattering like liberated monkeys. Miami Beach with an interesting accent.

And over in cool Fort Christian lay two freshly murdered corpses.

At the cemetery I turned down the Frenchtown road, dodged ruts and chuck holes until I was passing a cluster of Cha-Cha sheds. Built on concrete blocks, they looked more like outhouses than dwellings. Cha-Cha women in loose cotton garments with bony arms and pinched faces. The men in faded overalls and high straw hats. Frenchtown looked like a cut-rate setting for *Tobacco Road*.

Where the road opened up there was a two-story doorless building, the Normandie Bar. Beyond it the fishing docks. Bulbous rafts of water-lilies lay on the placid water. Turning around the building, I took the dirt road another hundred yards to the Casino.

It stood on a point of land, a gaunt gabled nightmare of a house with peeling paint and shutters hanging askew.

Braking the Volks, I got out and walked toward the front door. A cross of boards had been nailed to the frame. Grass poked up through warped porch boards. A big rat darted from under the house into the sunlight, blinked and scurried back. From the porch to the water's edge was a matter of twenty yards. Somewhere off in the water the body of Victor Polo had floated. Naked. I wondered what had happened to his clothes. The tangles of water-lily made the point a poor place for a midnight swim.

Offshore an open fishing boat put-putted away toward Hassel Island. Beside me a voice said, "Looking for something, mon?"

He was a short man in blue denims and a stained skivvy shirt that showed muscular arms. A man in his mid-thirties with a tanned round face that could have been an ad for Italian noodles. Instead of a Cha-Cha hat he wore a gray baseball cap. Stuck in the corner of his mouth was a stubby black cigar.

"Just looking," I said.

"Not much to look at."

"Agreed."

"A big place, once. Lights, people. That was when Polo ran it. Good times then."

"Five years ago," I said. "I came here a few times."

Turning he pulled off his cap and pointed toward the channel. "Yesterday morning Polo's body was floating out there. My pa towed it in."

"That's interesting," I said. "Suppose we drift over to the Normandie and nibble a couple."

He put back his hat and nodded. "It's about that time." His hand shot out and gripped mine. "Pierre Duroc," he said with the right French accent. "It'll be a pleasure."

The Normandie Bar was open on three sides for ventilation. Inside, round-topped tables with old wire-backed chairs. A long bar with a brass foot rail and stacked cases of liquor for take-out sales. Half a dozen men at the bar watching TV from San Juan. At the tables a cluster of beer-drinkers with leathery fishermen's skins. At two bits a shot it was a place where you could get a lot to drink for your money. Outside on the sun-baked clay, Negro children and Cha-Cha kids were playing ball. A mongrel dog yapped after the ball and nipped it before a kick sprawled him a yard away.

"Kids," Pierre said expansively. "I got three kids. How about you, mon?"

"I'm just a growing boy."

A shirt-sleeved bartender strolled over. Pierre ordered in French and I said, "Two fingers of iced rum."

"D'accord," the bartender said and went away.

Pierre took off his ball cap and fanned himself. Over in a dark corner an old Negro strummed disconnected chords on a battered guitar. He wore a red shirt, patched black trousers and he was barefoot. On his head a broken straw hat. Silvery stubble stood out against his black skin. He began to hum something unintelligible.

I said, "You were saying your pa found Polo yesterday."

Pierre nodded.

"How long had he been in the water?"

"Maybe since the night before."

"Much of a knife wound?"

He shook his head, turned and pointed at a table a few yards away. "We stretched him out there. Everyone had a good look. 'Course we put an apron over him first, being naked like he was."

"That was thoughtful."

He nodded again. "Polo didn't have too many friends around here."

"Enemies?"

"Everyone got enemies, mon."

"Women?"

"Everyone got a woman, too. Good girls tried to stay away from Polo. He had kind of a bad name."

"What way?"

"Couple girls he was sweet on went away. Some said he put them on a boat for South America. Maybe no. But the girls never came back."

The old Negro got up and shuffled over to us. He stuck out a skinny hand and I dropped a quarter in it. Doffing his hat, he swooped it down and around in a stately bow. Then he ambled over to the bar and ordered a beer.

"Henry," Pierre said. "You want him to play?"

"The bribe was for silence."

Pierre laughed. The bartender brought our drinks. Outside a car rattled up in a plume of dust. We bore into our drinks and from the corner of my eye I saw Big John come in and stride to the bar. The back of his shirt was plastered against his shoulder blades. He put both forearms on the bar and rested his weight on them. The back of his thick neck glistened with sweat.

Pierre was stirring ice in his glass. "You a friend of Polo's?"

"I never knew him. What brought him back?"

Pierre shrugged. "Maybe he want to sell the Casino."

I shook my head. The rum was so cold it was almost taste-less. In heat like this you could drink a lot of it without getting a hangover. A special tropic bonus for alcoholics. Pierre eased back in his chair and said, "He was in prison."

I opened my eyes wider. "Where?"

"Somewhere. In the States. The police tell me. Polo tried to rob a bank. He had bad luck." He picked up his drink and let a lot of it flow down his gullet. Wiping his mouth on the back of his wrist, he said, "That's news, huh?"

"It's news." It meant Polo had been broke when he left St. Thomas or he had gone broke shortly afterward. Kelly Martin had run into him in Las Vegas. He had been gambling and not winning, either. From Vegas he had come back to Charlotte Amalie, Frenchtown, and a knife in the heart.

I said, "Did he know Reba Royce?"

"Maybe. Everyone knew her. She had lotta friends. She had a Stateside millionaire, too. Everyone know that."

I winced. The whole town knew about Reba. Including Allegra. Sonny had been a good deal less than discreet.

The old Negro mumbled something to Big John. Big John turned slowly, stared at him and struck him across the face. Henry bounced against the bar, rolled along it and fell to the floor. Big John picked his guitar off the bar and tossed it after him. It hit with a dull strum. Henry crawled over to his hat, put it on carefully, picked up his guitar and pulled himself up. Without looking back, he tottered out of the door and disappeared. Voices picked up where they had left off.

I said, "Any guesses who killed Reba?"

Pierre picked up his glass and drained it. "It's been a real pleasure," he said. "Any time you wanta go fishing I got a boat. A good boat. Plenty fish the other side of Hassel Island." He stood up, hitched his pants and adjusted his ball cap. "Lunch time," he said. "The old woman's waiting for me. She don't like to be kept waiting."

"She probably looks forward to it," I said. "For the conversation."

He shot me a sardonic grin, turned and ambled out of the bar. Big John lifted a shot glass, downed it and called for another. I finished my drink, paid the bill and went out into the sunlight.

The kids had disappeared. The mongrel dog lay panting in the sparse shade. A man could get a drink in Frenchtown and that was about all. It was that kind of a place. I could have picked up as much information without leaving The Lodge.

Starting the Volks, I spun it around and drove past the Cha-Cha cabins, and out to the highway. I took Allegra's map from my pocket and turned up Frenchman's Hill.

It was dirt road all the way with loose stones and hairpin turns. From the high crest I peered down through jungle growth to the broad sand-edged claw of Magens Bay where aquamarine water lapped lazily at the chalk-white shoreline. A breeze stirred palm branches around me. I studied the map again and turned down the other side. After a while I scuttled up an access road arched over with branches and tropical creepers.

The road widened into a gravel turnaround in front of a green stucco cottage. Sonny's snuggery. There was a closed garage and a border of tropical plants. The aluminum window shutters were closed. The high tangle of branches overhead kept out all except a few shafts of sunlight. Parking the Volks, I got out and mopped my face. The air was close and damp. Mosquitoes hummed invisibly. I swatted my neck and killed one. Then I walked across the drive to the front door and turned the knob.

CHAPTER FIVE

The knob turned part way and hung. It was locked. I left the door and walked around the cottage. The kitchen door had an aluminum frame. It was locked, too. Bending down, I could see the beveled side of the door bolt. The wooden jamb had shrunk away from the aluminum door. With the Volks key, I pried at the bolt until it slid back enough to let me pull open the door.

I went inside and let the door snap shut behind me.

The kitchen stank damply of tropical rot. Moisture had swelled the wood paneling and spotted the varnish with black mold. Ceiling paper had swung down from the plaster in patches. There were beer cans in the sink and a fuzz of purple mold grew in a dirty milk bottle. I moved into the living room and snapped on a light.

The modernistic furniture was island-made and cheap. Varnished wooden legs and wild tropical patterns on the nubby fabrics. There was a radio and a TV and a small bar faced with white imitation leather. Shelves behind the bar held a reasonable supply of liquor. On a table lay some copies of *Paris-Match*. The newest Island newspaper was a month old. One wall showed a damp patch in the plaster. One heavy rain and the plaster would drop off the wall.

Walking over the straw throw rugs, I went into a bedroom. The ceiling light showed a mussed double bed and a vanity table with powders and perfumes. There was a shower and a woman's shower cap and a tumble of used bath towels. An assortment of bottles in the wall medicine cabinet. In the closet a pair of man's bath slippers and a dressing gown of beige Japanese silk. I turned on a faucet and got a trickle of rusty water. A thirty-thousand-dollar house decaying and reverting to the jungle around it.

The smaller bedroom held a single bed and a bare mattress, nothing more. I went back into the larger bedroom and opened the chest of drawers. Hairpins and a rusted curling iron, an empty Kleenex box, some facial creams and a stack of mildewed linen. The damp air was chill with the ghosts of love long dead.

Beside the vanity stood a woven wastebasket. Sorting through wads of lipsticked cotton, I came across a crumple of paper. Smoothing it on the glass top, I saw it was a penciled note: *Back on Saturday.* I put it in my pocket and went back to the living room, wondering if Sonny had come back that Saturday or if the assignation had never been kept. Reba would never tell.

Shivering a little, I turned out the light and walked through the kitchen and let myself out the back door. As the door clicked shut I heard the sounds of a car on the road below. Sprinting for the Volks, I slid inside and waited tensely until the sound of the car died away.

Slapping at a vicious host of mosquitoes, I started the Volks and skidded down the drive to the mountain road, turning back toward Charlotte Amalie. Twenty minutes later I was pulling into Dominic's.

Kelly opened her door part way and stood there, surprise on her face. She was wearing a fitted poplin skirt, a filmy neckerchief, a violet blouse and leather sandals. There were sleep crescents under her eyes and her cheeks looked slightly hollow. "Hello, Steve," she said tightly. "What is it?"

"It's high noon," I said. "I got to thinking we might share some gin and little cakes. If you haven't lunched yet, that is."

Her chin lifted slightly. "I'm awfully sorry. I've already made a date."

"Dominic?—not that it's any of my business."

She turned and nudged the door the rest of the way open. In a lounge chair, smoking a cigarette, sat Simon Hargrave, looking as if he had just made himself another million.

"Well, well," he gloated, "the poor man's Philo Vance. Sonny's been looking for you."

"Yeah? Where is he?"

"Free for the moment—no thanks to you. Up at The Lodge."

Kelly was making a big thing of not meeting my eyes.

"How convenient for everyone," I murmured. "What persuaded the police to turn him loose?"

Hargrave crossed his legs comfortably and gave me an expansive smile. "It was the knife. The same knife that killed Reba killed Victor Polo. Sonny couldn't have killed Polo so that lets him out."

"Why couldn't he have killed Polo?"

Hargrave leaned forward and his voice grew unpleasant. "Because the night Polo was killed Sonny's covered for every minute."

I laughed shortly. "You were the one who figured he'd knifed Reba, not me. But I made a mistake, too." I glanced at Kelly. "It won't happen again. Uh uh."

"Steve," she said tautly, "I—"

"Save it," I snapped. "Save it for the new client." Turning, I walked back along the corridor to the bar and got up on a stool. Dominic was sitting at a porch table reading a paper. The breeze flapped the loose edges and Dominic straightened them and peered across at me. When he had memorized my face he went back to his paper. A very cool customer, Mr. Ralph Dominic. Cooler than midnight in Little America. To Dominic a knife would be an old friend. Slip-blades, toad-stabbers and sharp stilettos. They matched his personality.

The bartender slid a rum collins across the bar and stuck a couple of plastic straws in it. I pulled them out, bent them and dropped them on the floor. The bartender was peeling an orange with a short black-handled knife. It was the kind of knife I had seen sticking out of Reba's back last night. Twenty cents apiece in a thousand dime stores. No class, but for a weapon a bargain.

I drank my rum and stared out at the waterfront where an old lugger was casting off, taking advantage of the breeze. Its shabby sails flapped and filled, the jib tautened and the boat nosed around into the channel. I thought of my ketch tied to a buoy at the foot of Maine Avenue in Washington and found myself wishing I were boarding her right now. Lifting my glass, I stared across the rim and said, "Here's luck, Violet Eyes. This time hold out for a ring."

The bartender laid down his orange and moved over to me. "You said something?"

"Just talking to myself."

He looked at me curiously and went back to his work.

Dominic yawned, stretched and folded the paper. He got up and sauntered over behind the bar. From the shelf he took a bottle of scotch and poured himself three fingers worth. He added ice and a jet of soda and rotated it. Then he leaned back and drank, looking out at the water broodingly.

A Hillman convertible turned in off the promenade and bore down on us. It stopped outside the yard and a girl got out. A tall girl wearing a flouncy tropical skirt and matching halter bra. There was a colored silk handkerchief around her hair. Sybil Dominic. She walked quickly into the room and laid her hands on the bar. Dominic watched her, his face immobile.

"Honey," she said pleadingly, "can't you be nice to me any more? Not even a little?"

His thick lips curled. "I told you to keep the old bitch outa here. I'm telling you again, baby. Next time I'll bust her nose open. She's got the whole town laughin' at me. I won't put up with it no longer."

Sybil bit her lips and looked down. "I know," she said apologetically, "but that's mother. She insists on coming with me and I can't stop her."

Dominic moved against the bar and put his hands on it. "Tell you what you do then, baby. Stay the hell outa here yourself. That'll solve everything."

Her eyes lifted mistily. "Ralph—I love you. You know I do. Can't we try again? I mean—"

His eyes had narrowed cruelly. He called her a filthy name. Sybil recoiled as though he had slapped her. White spots spread over her cheekbones. She shook her head dazedly and murmured, "I don't care what you call me. I only know I love you. Ralph, if you don't come back to me I'll …" Her voice drifted away.

"You'll *what*, baby?"

Her body stiffened. Her face lifted bravely and she said, "I'll tell what I know about you and Polo. Why he came back."

Dominic's face contorted with fury. His hands closed into hamlike fists. "You better not," he snarled. "One bleat outa you and you're likely to end up the same way he did."

"And Reba," she challenged. "I could tell *that* story, too."

He called her another vile name. Her body shuddered and her fist went to her mouth. Teeth sank into the knuckles. Tears swelled on her cheeks like big translucent pearls. For a moment she wavered before him and then she spun around and ran out. I watched her get into the Hillman and roar away.

Dominic's face was the face of a sick man. He stared at his fists and with an effort made them relax. Picking up his glass, he downed the rest of his drink and began mixing another.

I said, "Any cover charge for the show?"

Turning slowly, he glowered at me. "Oh," he said. "Sonny's pal. Nobody asked you back, pal. How about dusting off?"

"Grade-C dialogue," I said. "But from you even that much would be an effort."

He set down his glass carefully and stalked over to me. "Meaning what?"

"Easy on the heavy menace," I warned. "You'll have me all nervous and trembling. Then you might think you could get away with calling me a dirty name."

He called me one.

By then I was off the stool, both feet solidly on the floor. My left hand caught his shirt at the neckline. I jerked him hard against the bar and slapped his face. Spots of pink colored his olive skin. He tried to shake free but he was off balance. His right arm shot across the bar but I grabbed a heavy ash tray and smashed it on his fist. He yelped and fell back, ripping his shirt. Reaching behind him for a bottle, he vaulted over the bar and came at me. I picked up a chair and rammed it into his face. His feet went up and his body dropped backward. Blood was spurting out of his nose. One hand covered his face as he rolled from side to side, moaning. I put half a dollar on the bar and finished my drink.

The corridor door opened and Kelly walked out followed by Hargrave. They stared down at Dominic as they crossed the dance floor.

Hargrave said nervously, "*You* did it?"

"Born and bred in the briar patch, Br'er Fox."

"For God's sake why?"

"Our host got a little yippy. At a time when I was spoiling for a fight." I stared at Hargrave until he was across the floor and out on the porch. Kelly didn't look back.

The Negro came around from behind the bar, a wet towel in his hand. He looked nervously at me and bent down to mop Dominic's bloody face. Dominic cursed him. With quiet dignity the Negro got up and walked away. When he was behind the bar again, I said, "If anyone calls the law I trust you'll remember how all this got started."

"I surely will," he said, picked out another orange and began peeling it.

I walked out through the porch and into the sunlight. Behind me I could hear Dominic shouting at the bartender. From beside the building a pink Mercedes convertible snaked out toward the promenade. Hargrave's car and Kelly beside him. The sun glasses she was wearing would help Hargrave look only fifty or so. If age was bothering anyone.

Out in the channel the old lugger was under full sail. I got heavily into the Volks and drove along the promenade and up the hill to The Lodge.

CHAPTER SIX

Sonny and I were alone on the veranda. Alone except for the parrot poaching at the popcorn dish. Sonny's face had a rum flush and he was in a surly mood. "Damn insolent of those police to question me so damn long."

I started my second hamburger and said nothing.

"You sure it was only ten when I pulled out last night? Seemed a hell of a lot later to me."

"You were carrying a heavy cargo, skipper."

He shook his head wearily and stared at his scraped knuckles. "They're crazy if they think I ever had anything to do with that mulata wench."

"I'd go a little easy on that line," I suggested. "Last night at Dominic's a roomful of people saw you grab Reba. And heard you plead with her."

"*Plead.*"

"Sounded like."

"Jesus Christ, Steve!"

"I'm your friend," I said. "I also know about the cottage on Crown Mountain. Reba's Roost."

Licking his lips, he stared at me. Suddenly his face looked lost and hopeless. "How?"

"They were talking about it over in Frenchtown."

He buried his face in his hands. "I must have been crazy. Now they'll say I killed her."

"They're saying it already."

His hand hit the canvas seat cushion. "Why?"

"The thought's so juicy it's irresistible. They know you bought Reba the Crown Mountain cottage, they know you lived with her—weekends, anyway." I took the note from my pocket, smoothed it on the table and handed it to him. "I got this out of the bedroom wastebasket."

His hand reached for it and he studied it dumbly. Handing it back he said, "I never wrote that."

"Positive?"

"I'd swear it. It's not my handwriting. Oh, I left notes for her now and then—no phone up there—but not that one."

Folding the note, I put it in my billfold. "Was anyone else playing house with her—or shouldn't I ask?"

"How the hell would I know?" he asked bitterly. "A girl like that could have had a dozen lovers without my knowing it." He looked at me. "I guess I'm getting what I asked for."

"Start beating your breast and you'll get plenty of volunteer pummeling from the townsfolk, so let's keep the moral recriminations out of it. The wench is dead; you didn't kill her. Someone did. The problem is finding out who."

"Thank God for a logical mind," he muttered and tilted his glass. Then he got up, tramped over to the bar and mixed another drink. Elbows on the bar, he stared at the overhead and said, "If the same knife killed Reba and Victor Polo that means the same murderer."

"Uh uh. It only means the same man could have killed them both—if the same knife was used. But it's a common kind of knife—you've probably got four or five of them here between the kitchen and the bar. In short the wound would be fairly easy to duplicate—by anyone who knew about Polo's murder and wanted to take the trouble."

"I hadn't thought of that."

I lighted a cigarette and blew smoke at the feeding parrot. It blinked and glared at me balefully.

I said, "Let's hope the bloodstains turn out to be yours."

"Of course they will."

"They'll have to send the cloth to San Juan for lab tests. If they do it today they'll get word back tomorrow or the next day."

"That's one thing I'm not worried about."

"Good. What did Reba wear on her ring finger?"

"Nothing.

"You never gave her a ring?"

He shifted uneasily. "Well, I gave her a topaz once but I never knew what she did with it. I suppose she could have had it made into a ring. Is it important?"

"Her ring finger was hacked off. But that could have been to develop a robbery motive."

He shook his head slowly. "I can't believe she's dead. Not Reba. There was so much life in her. And that marvelous young body…" He lifted his glass morosely.

"To change the subject slightly, did Victor Polo ever have a reputation as a procurer?"

"A pimp? There's no prostitution here. Too many unattached female tourists eager for anything in pants."

"That doesn't rule anything out. Vice rings aren't just the stuff of sensational journalism, they exist. To feed them they need girls. Young, pretty girls in all shapes and colors. Around these islands about all a native girl can look forward to is being a wash woman, a maidservant or a taxi-driver's wife—if she's lucky. You know these parts, I don't. But I was thinking these islands might be a pretty good source of supply for the kind of girls who get into that kind of racket."

"Could be."

"There's always a man, though. Smooth and a fast talker, with plenty of dough to throw around and impress the girls. Gambling and women are closer than bourbon and branchwater. Over in Frenchtown a Cha-Cha intimated that Polo had a bad name where women were concerned—in the sort of way we're talking about."

He shrugged. "Polo was a mystery man. All kinds of stories about him if you wanted to listen. I wasn't that interested."

I said, "A professional gambler is a man who's basically lazy—so's a professional procurer who lives on a whore's earnings. A gambler has the same cold and cynical approach to life that a pimp has. And both of them have fewer sentiments than a newt's hind toe. Polo wouldn't have come back here because of any woman he left behind five years ago—and the chances are he didn't leave any behind. I think he came back because he was down on his luck and he thought he could raise some money in Saint Thomas. Easy or hard."

Sonny blinked at me dully.

"Maybe that gives us more to work on than just Reba's murder does. A robber could have killed her or a disappointed lover—none of that leads anywhere. But with Polo we can rough it down to money. Or so it looks."

Sonny ran his hand through his hair distractedly. "I can't think straight. All I know is I didn't kill Reba. I wanted her to quit dancing—she wouldn't. We had fights over it and finally broke up. She cleared out of the house and I never went back. I thought Dominic had taken her over."

"Who says he didn't?"

Someone was marching up the steps outside. I turned and saw a middle-aged woman in a shapeless sun dress. Her white hair was bobbed and her face was pink with exertion. Mrs. Vane Drury, the third member of the Coco Island triumvirate. "Sonny Tyner," she called imperiously, "you have an elevator installed or I swear I'll never come here again."

She shuffled onto the porch and sagged against the railing, fanning herself and gasping. Finally she recovered, blinked like a plump toad and stared at me. "Who's this?"

"Steve Bentley," Sonny said.

"When did he get in?"

"Yesterday, Vane. Do you want a drink?"

"Why wasn't I told?"

"My fault," I said. "Yesterday I wasn't in presentable condition."

She got up, came over to me and extended a damp hand. I took it briefly. "You look plenty presentable today," she said. "Have you met my Sybil yet?"

"I've seen her."

"Attractive girl, isn't she?—Steve, did you say?"

"Yes, ma'am. Very attractive."

"She's a divorcée, too—or will be when they finish their damn paper shuffling down at the courthouse." She glanced over at Sonny. "Light rum—by that I'm talking about color only. A double shot. Hell, you know how I take it." She settled down beside me. "Where'd you see Sybil? She didn't tell me."

"She didn't notice me. It happened to be at Dominic's."

"When?"

"Last night."

"We went there together," Sonny explained.

She reared back and stared over at him. "I'm surprised a friend of yours would let you disgrace yourself the way you did last night."

"I did it all on my own," Sonny said wearily. "Let's change the subject."

"How did the police treat you?"

"Reasonably badly."

"What does Allegra have to say about all this?"

"Very little."

She took her glass from Sonny and settled back again. Tilting the drink, she let half of it slide down her throat. Smacking her lips, she purred. "That was almost worth the climb. Anyway I feel marvelous. Somebody laid Dominic out—right smack in front of his bar."

Sonny smiled.

Mrs. Drury said, "Whoever he was I want to pin a medal on him."

"You'll never be closer," Sonny said.

Turning she stared at me. "You! Young man, you've got a life-long friend in Vane Drury."

"That's kind of you," I said. "Whether my motives were creditable or not is another thing."

"Doesn't matter a damn. The point is, you did it. That shows it can be done. Now there'll be others." She looked up and chortled wickedly. "They'll make his life hell on earth." Patting the back of my hand, she said, "I ought to get Sybil over here right this minute. You're not only too good to be true, you're Heaven's answer to an old woman's prayer. Sonny, you're responsible if he leaves Saint Thomas."

"Don't eat him alive, Vane. Since you're here we might as well talk a little business."

"Very well. Too bad Simon can't be found. I've been calling him for hours."

"He's off on a tour of the Island," I said. "With a young person."

Sonny's eyebrows lifted.

"Kelly," I muttered.

Mrs. Drury belched, patted her chest and rumbled, "Simon's an old ass, if you ask me."

"Nobody's asked you yet."

"I'm free to express my opinion among friends." She drank heartily, smacked her lips and put down the nearly empty glass. "We won't say anything about that murdered mulata wench, Sonny, we'll just discuss business. But if anyone asks me, it was Ralph Dominic who killed her."

"There's a husky slander law on the statutes," I said.

"Don't be prissy. If you knew how I hated that man you'd let me rant without protest."

"It was just a passing thought," I murmured.

The parrot had caught her roving eyes. "Dreadful thieving beast," she hissed. "If it nips me just once more I'll throttle it."

Sonny sat down on a hassock in front of us. "Shall we get down to business?"

We did. For half an hour. Mrs. Drury doing most of the talking. When I finally got a chance I described some of the tax advantages we could build into the corporate structure of Coco Island. After that Mrs. Drury said, "Sonny, this sensible young man has my entire confidence. Anything he thinks ought to be done has my vote."

I said, "Mr. Hargrave may be less co-operative."

"Pooh," she breathed. "Sonny and I make a majority on this particular board of directors, so don't give Simon a second thought. Also, you are dining at my home this evening."

I glanced at Sonny for help. Sonny said calmly, "He can't, Vane. Steve's dining at Government House tonight."

"Tomorrow night, then." She struggled off the sofa, fanned herself briefly and said, "I'll be down at Mike's Bar for the next several hours."

"Getting drunk?" Sonny asked. "Hell, you can do that right here."

"No," she sniffed. "Keeping my long ears open to find out what they're saying about you."

Sonny's face set. "I don't particularly want to know."

"*I* do. Well, give my respects to the Governor—you lying bastards!" She crossed the porch and began descending the steps. When the sounds died away I said, "I'll bet she fights double her weight in torpedo boats."

"Armored cruisers," Sonny said. "That's a remarkable old girl. Her husband lost all their money, died and left her with a baby girl and a mortgage on their house. So Vane came down here, started her real-estate business, and made herself a million dollars faster than you can count it. What do you think about her?"

"I think she'd do well to let Sybil live her own life."

"With *Dominic?*"

"With the butcher's apprentice, if she wants."

The parrot had devastated the popcorn dish. It was preening itself and watching me carefully. I got up, lighted a cigarette and blew smoke over the porch railing. The harbor water was at slack tide, listless and coppery. Over near the tip of Hassel Island a sloop lay becalmed. It would be brutally hot out there under the implacable sun.

Sonny said, "Restless?"

"A mite. I think I'll drift down into town and probe the pulse of private opinion."

"Whatever that amounts to."

There were footsteps from the house and Allegra came out onto the veranda. Looking at me she said, "Steve, would you mind...?"

"I was just leaving." Pulling my sun glasses from my pocket I put them on and trotted down the long staircase to the road. The seat of the Volks was hotter than a branding iron. I spread a beach towel over it, got in and bounced down the hill toward Frenchtown.

When I got there the Normandie Bar hadn't changed, only the cast of characters. A couple of tall, blond, sunburned men who looked like Danes in one corner, Henry, the old guitar player, was sleeping at a table and a clutch of overalled Cha-Chas rolled dice at the bar. I stepped up to the bar and ordered a bottle of Heineken's.

The bartender pulled one out of a bin of ice chips and uncapped it. The beer was cold enough to freeze your teeth. The bartender went over to the TV and fiddled with the dials. No response. The bartender swore softly, picked up a paper and studied the San Juan track entries. Flies buzzed and crawled over beery table tops. Henry snored and scratched his chin in his sleep. A lively, invigorating place. I wondered what the hell I was doing there.

Beside me a voice said, "You move around a lot, Mr. Bentley—for a new arrival."

"It's a free country, or so they say." I turned and saw a tall man in a white short-sleeved shirt, white ducks and white shoes. His face was tan and the ends of his hair were bleached from sun.

"It's a free country, all right," he said and his hand dipped into his hip pocket.

"Hold it," I said. "You're going to pull out red, white and blue credentials with Edgar's signature on it and enlist my co-operation. Consider it done."

"You happen to be right," he said in a surprised voice. "So I'd appreciate anything you might care to pass along about your friend Mr. Tyner."

"I can imagine. It just happens I haven't anything to pass along."

"He's in a serious spot."

"Relax," I said. "Have a drink."

"On duty," he said soberly. "Well, maybe a Coke."

The bartender pricked up his ears, dug into the ice chips and uncapped a Coke bottle.

I said, "I hadn't heard you'd been called into the case yet."

He put his bottle down and grimaced. "I haven't been."

"But you expect to be?"

"I expect to be."

"Fine. That'll give you the official standing you don't have at the moment. Drop around then and we'll have a chat."

He smiled slowly. "There's another case in which I enjoy official standing, Mr. Bentley—the murder of Victor Polo."

I tilted my bottle, guzzled pleasurably and set it down on the bar. "That's a bird of a different feather."

"Quite different. Polo was a parolee from a Federal penitentiary. He broke parole by leaving the States and coming here. That put me in the case. No invitation needed."

I shook out a cigarette and lighted it. Leaning my elbows on the bar, I said, "Polo was dead before I got here. That sums up my knowledge of his murder."

"In less than twenty-four hours there was another killing. I'm inclined to think there's a connection. What's your opinion?"

"Everything's possible. But so far I haven't heard of any link being established."

He lifted his bottle and drained it slowly. Then he wiped his lips and said, "When Polo's body was found it was naked. What happened to his clothes was a logical question. Now they've turned up. Interested?"

"Mildly."

"An old Cha-Cha was picked up down at the market wearing them. He bought them from a Negro—for seventy-five cents."

"A bargain."

"Wasn't it? The Negro admitted selling them. Said he found them in a trash can."

"Where?"

The tall man smiled again. "Over near the waterfront, Mr. Bentley—and directly in back of the little house where Reba Royce lived."

CHAPTER SEVEN

Late in the afternoons the Thomians come down to their beaches, when the flat heat of the sun has begun to fade and the lightest possible breeze begins to breathe onshore. I was sitting in an aluminum beach chair, sipping a tall one and staring out over Sapphire Bay toward Shark Island. The bathers were staying close to shore and looking around themselves carefully. Earlier, kids with masks and spearguns had brought in two moray eels from the coral beds just offshore. The eels had bodies like bars of white iron and jaws like skinned foxes. Before the eels had been speared I had donned flippers and Scuba tanks and cruised around the coral beds looking for lobsters in coral holes. The kids had been looking for lobsters, too. What they had found were morays. So much for underwater sports.

Then Sybil Dominic had driven up in her Hillman, taken a long swim and dried herself in the sun. Now she was standing at the pavilion's bar, drinking rum on the rocks. She had a swimmer's body, streamlined and long-muscled. Her hips and waist were slim and her breasts were small and compact. From what I could see of her there was little that even a specialist like Dominic could complain of—unless, possibly, she had outsize feet. And in the folklore of puberty that was supposed to mean something lascivious.

A woman with a small child passed the time of day with Sybil Dominic, a darkly tanned, bearded man went over to the bar and had a drink with her. Then they went away. Sybil finished her drink, signed a bar chit and turned around. At first she gazed out at the island-spotted horizon, then her gaze shortened and rested on me. She studied me for a while and then she came unsteadily from the bar.

Halting beside me, she leaned forward, braced an arm on the back of my chair and said, "Is your name Bentley?"

"Yes."

Her free hand came up and slapped the side of my face. Blinking, I rubbed my cheek. "What was that for?"

"For what you did to Ralph. I can fight my own battles—I don't need or want anyone defending me." Her face was flushed and her lips moved loosely.

I said, "You're presuming a lot, Mrs. Dominic. Your little spat with Dominic only established the atmosphere. What followed had little if anything to do with you. That slap would have been better spent on your husband."

With an effort she straightened up and stood swaying slightly. "I happen to love my husband."

"There's no accounting for tastes, but if your mother would slack off my guess is you'd drop him like a blowfish."

Her eyes narrowed. "What do you mean?"

"By marrying Dominic—by hanging around him now— you're punishing your mother for God only knows what. Maybe just to show her you're of age and not a child any longer."

"Analyzing me?" she sneered.

"The slap buys me that much."

She put her hands on her hips. They were beautiful hands with small wrists and long artist's fingers. "I'll thank you to forget all about me, Mr. Bentley."

"That might take a little doing."

She peered at me. "How do you mean that?"

"Some people would take it as a compliment. Depending on their frame of mind—and their complexes."

Her lips moved uncertainly and she cocked her head. "Amateur psychologists," she grated finally. "God, what bores."

"You could pay more for a lot less."

"A matter of opinion," she muttered, swayed and lifted one arm to her forehead. "I feel lousy."

"That's what rum can do on a hot day." I got up. "Let's go dangle our toesies in the water."

Her eyes widened, she stared at me and said, "Hell, why not?"

As we stepped down from the concrete platform, I took her arm in case she decided to fall. She moved unsteadily across the slanting sand to the water's edge. Then she sat down and stretched out her long legs. I sat down beside her. Her face turned toward me and she murmured, "I guess mother prejudiced me against you. She thinks you're the answer to a maiden's prayer."

"Your mother's at an impressionable age. And she makes snap judgments."

"You're a friend of Sonny's."

I nodded.

She bit her lips. One hand dug into the wet sand, lifted a clot and squeezed it through her fingers. "You don't think he killed Reba?"

"Do you?"

She shook her head. "I don't want to think so. But people are saying it already. God, how I hate this rotten little town."

"Towns are pretty much the same."

She shrugged. "This is the only town I know. Where I was raised. It's what I call home." She laughed bitterly.

I said, "In addition to the talk that Sonny killed Reba there's some sentiment holding that her death and Victor Polo's are tied together."

Her brown eyes were the size of chestnuts. "I don't believe it. Victor Polo came back here to—" She bit her lip and looked away.

"To what? Get another grubstake?"

"I don't know," she said tightly.

"You're lying. You told your husband you could tell why Polo came back. The fact that you haven't means you're protecting someone—Dominic."

She turned on me furiously. "You don't know anything about it! You don't know Ralph ...."

"I know his kind."

Drawing in her legs, she rose to her knees.

I said, "Calling me names won't solve anything, beautiful. Polo was your husband's partner. When the Casino was closed down Polo got out of town. Dominic didn't. Why not? What happened to their money? Did each one get a fair split? Is that why Polo came back? Or did he have something on Dominic worth money to a blackmailer?"

Abruptly she jumped up. I gazed at her taut face and said, "Just because Sonny's free now doesn't mean he's not under a lot of suspicion. This morning the police found Polo's clothes. They'd been stuffed in a trash barrel behind Reba's house. That's a circumstantial link between the two killings. So if you know anything about Polo's murder the time to blurt it out is now. Before gossip destroys what's left of Sonny's name."

Her hands clenched into small hard fists. Suddenly she whirled and ran toward the pavilion, her feet kicking back little plumes of sand. People watched her go, then turned and stared at me. I got up, waded into the water and swam over toward the tip of the beach. Pulling myself out, I climbed up on the sand, shook myself and sat on a rock until I was dry again. Then I trudged out to where I had parked the Volks. Sybil's Hillman was gone and so were most of the other cars. The sun was low over the edge of the water, glowing like the arc of an acetylene torch. Behind the bar the Negro was locking bottles away for the night. A Negress swept down the littered cement floor, humming snatches of some vagrant Caribbean melody.

A complicated lady, Mrs. Sybil Dominic. Almost a case study. I got into the Volks, turned around and headed back toward town.

The bar had high cavern ceilings. It was dark and cool and as damp as a mushroom cave. Years ago the walls had been rough-plastered and painted to look like hewn rock. What light there was filtered from hidden colored bulbs. Ivy and ferns trailed down from niches in the phony rock. The bartender was an aging blonde with wrinkled skin the color of a slug's belly. She wore a flimsy version of an evening dress and so did the pair of wait-resses. There wasn't much business and the waitresses were doing considerable chattering to each other.

Sitting on a bar stool was a handsome brown-skinned woman with broad shoulders and the proud aquiline face of a Carib Indian. Her breasts seemed to begin at her collar bone, swell outward, around and under like large hills. Either that or she was smuggling watermelons. She held her cigarette in an eight-inch golden stem. Her lacquered black hair glinted like shiny coal. According to my waitress she was the mistress of a deposed Caribbean dictator who was off somewhere else orga-nizing a counterrevolution. I could think of a lot less comfortable places to wait out a counterrevolution than St. Thomas. However the battle swung, I had the idea she would saunter off a winner.

Half-hidden in the dimness a honeymoon couple sprawled at a wall table, whispering and cooing and tossing off rum and grenadine as though it were Dr. Pepper. I was grateful for the distance between my table and the viscous baby talk. Through the louvered door tripped a tall youth with the head and frame of a skinny panther. His thick wavy hair had been streaked with bleach and he walked as lightly as if he had a cushion of air under his rubber soles. Real beat. He draped himself across a bar stool. The blond bartender mixed him something cold with red and green layers. Wavy Head stabbed a tentative tongue at the concoction, smiled distantly and got down to work. I didn't want to know what the drink was. From where I sat I could see it would burn holes in the skull the morning after. The Indian lady measured him with a sidelong glance and granted him a tolerant sneer. No danger there; no fun either. Hell, it was still the shank of the evening.

I stared at the uneven wall and decided the place had been designed by a refugee from the Pennsylvania coal fields. It had everything except a canary to prove the oxygen content. About midnight, when the walls began to sweat, you strapped on your helmet and safety lamp and stumbled home.

A girl pushed through the swinging doors and walked to the bar. She wore flat leather sandals with ankle thongs, a billowy cotton skirt and an off-the-shoulder white blouse. Her dark hair was parted in the middle and drawn behind her head with a big silver clip. She leaned toward the blond bartender and they conversed a few moments before the blonde shook her head and went back to polishing highball glasses. The girl looked around uncertainly, peered at the vacant tables and saw me, Her expression changed slightly and she came toward me in a flat-footed jungle walk. Sybil Dominic.

When she reached my table she leaned forward, flattening her palms on the table top and said, "Have you seen Vane—my mother?"

"She was said to be over at Mike's sampling the specialty of the house."

"Whatever that is. No, I've come from Mike's. She left there some time ago. I guess she'd had a lot to drink."

"That would sort of be her privilege."

Her eyes flashed. "Not to the point of making a fool of herself."

"Look who's talking."

She straightened, eyes narrow and arms tense. I said, "Relax, beautiful. I've stowed away enough grog that I don't slap so good, so let's forget that one. All I pointed out was that what's feed for the gosling can be dessert for the goose as well."

"I being the gosling, I suppose." She pulled out the chair facing me and eased herself into it. "You've got a point there. Why don't you buy me a drink?"

I flagged a waitress. She sauntered over and said, "Hi, Syb—what'll it be? The usual?"

Sybil nodded. The waitress went away and propped her elbows on the bar. It was one hell of a cool coal mine. I said, "If you catch up with Vane, don't mention you saw me."

"Why not?"

I shrugged. "According to Sonny we're dining with the Governor tonight." I picked up my drink and glanced across the rim at her. "Hi, Governor."

She laughed. Then she said, "I'm afraid I can't help liking you."

"People have tried making careers of not liking me. The odds are against them."

"Heavily. Cigarette?"

I handed her one and lighted it. She leaned back, inhaled and blew smoke toward the high ceiling. Her neck was long and youthful. I could see her swathed in silver mink under a Broadway marquee or stepping into an oyster-white Chrysler in a full-page color ad. I said, "Why didn't you break away from Saint Thomas?"

Her head lowered and she shrugged lightly. "Inertia, I guess. That and a strong-willed mother."

The waitress brought Sybil a highball.

"How much longer before your divorce comes through?"

"It depends. Vane's using all her influence to hurry it along. I'm doing what I can to slow it down."

"I see. How's Dominic?"

She frowned. "I shouldn't be sitting here drinking with a man who beat up my husband."

"I know," I said. "Ethics and morality are all against it. Besides, the whole town'll talk."

"The trouble is I find myself not really caring a hell of a lot."

"That's a healthy sign."

"So Vane would say." Turning, she glanced at the bar. "I suppose I ought to call the house and see if she's arrived there yet."

"Hell," I said, "let her have her fling. It's time the two of you stopped cosseting each other and settled down to a sensible relationship."

She turned back, picked up her glass and turned it slowly against the palm of her hand. "You're right, of course. But habit's a hard thing to fight—particularly in as small an area as this." Her eyes lifted. "Was Ralph really sleeping with Reba Royce?"

"Ask him."

"I have."

"I'll bet he told you to mind your own business."

"A good deal more vulgarly. So I assume he was."

"Well," I said, "the two of you are more or less separated so you could regard it as adultery on the half-shell."

"I suppose I could. Any more advice?"

"Not at the moment." I leered at the waitress and she drifted across the floor, preening her hair with one hand. "Two more drinks," I said. "On the half-shell."

"Huh?"

"You heard the man," Sybil said archly.

The waitress put her hands on her hips, gave an exaggerated shrug and wandered back to the bar. I decided to let her solve her problem her own way.

Sybil said quietly, "You're really a detective, aren't you?"

I blinked and sat up in my chair. My shoulders were developing a rum slouch. I said, "I am not a detective or anything like one. What I am is a certified public accountant—a dull trade by most standards—a nonpracticing lawyer and a tax consultant. What I know about criminal work comes from a couple of years with the CID in Korea, and from some time before that with Internal Revenue. Who gave you the bum steer?"

"Mother. Sonny told her you'd been involved in solving a lot of cases around Washington."

"Largely by chance involvement. Or you can reconcile it with the fact that I deal with money—often in large amounts—and money or its substitutes is the basis for most crime."

"Then you're really here just to help out with the Coco Isle Corporation, nothing else?" Her voice sounded disappointed.

"Strange as it may seem."

The waitress brought our drinks and took away our empty glasses, glaring suspiciously at me and flouncing off to the bar where the Indian lady and the blondined beatnik were rolling dice. While we had been drinking the tables had filled gradually and the bartender had put a scratchy record on a pickup behind the bar. Through cheap ceiling speakers the sound was strictly Low-Fi, but when you had pickled your eardrums in Cruzan rum for a couple of years it didn't make a hell of a lot of difference.

Simon Hargrave came in, raised his hand over his eyes as though he were Columbus sighting the West Indies and scanned the clientele. When he caught sight of us he walked quickly over and said, "Syb, your mother's at the house."

"Drunk or sober?"

"In between."

Sybil raised her glass and let most of it slide down her beautiful gullet. Setting down the glass, she sighed. "I suppose I ought to go back."

"I'll go with you," I offered.

Hargrave said, "I want to talk with you, Bentley."

"It's past office hours."

"I'll pay overtime," he sneered.

Sybil stood up a little unevenly. "Don't fight, boys. Simon, you're too old, and, Steve, you've done enough fighting for one day. Thanks for the drinks and the chat. See you around."

She spiraled slowly out of the chair and weaved toward the swinging doors. I watched the doors open and close behind her.

Then I looked up at Hargrave. He said, "I don't mind telling you I don't like your type, Bentley."

"Just what would my type be?"

His mouth opened and closed. He had been about to say something and he had thought better of it. Much better.

"Well?" I said.

His mouth clicked shut. He grimaced irritably and said, "It's worth money to me to have you out of Saint Thomas. How much?"

"My price?" I looked down at my glass and nudged it along the table with one knuckle. "What would be your idea of my price, Mr. Hargrave?"

"A thousand dollars?"

I smiled tolerantly.

"Fifteen hundred."

Shaking my head, I said, "I came here in a professional capacity. There's my fee to think of."

"How much?"

"About five thousand," I said. "Maybe more."

"All right, damn you."

I stood up. "Fine. We'll go up and talk to Sonny about it."

His mouth opened.

"Something wrong? Sonny's one-third of the Corporation. And he's my friend. Shouldn't we do him the courtesy of telling him about your proposal?"

His face looked like gray stone. "That wasn't part of it. It's not healthy around here for you. I was giving you a chance to clear out quietly and profitably."

"I'm in favor of it. To a small-timer like me five G's is a lot of money. But there's Sonny's angle to consider."

The cords in his throat stood out like guy wires. "I'm telling you to get out."

"My heart's in my mouth, Hargrave. You're not big enough to scare me and you're not smart enough to worry me. You're just another rich ageing man nursing the frayed illusion that money's the answer to everything. Now take your five thousand dollars and scamper back to one of your fancy women. Tell her I'm a brute if it'll comfort you. I don't mind."

His face was puffy with rage. His fingers curled and uncurled like loose springs. The scratchy phono record had stopped. The bartender, the waitresses and a lot of eyes were watching us. Everyone except the Indian lady and the gaunt youth. But for the click of dice the room was silent. Suddenly Hargrave spun around and stalked toward the swinging doors. He slammed into them and out into the night. I ran a finger inside my collar and sat down. The loudspeaker began to blare another tune, equally scratchy. I rattled ice in my drink and finished it. When I looked at the bar again the feline youth was laying some money in the palm of the Indian lady. She looked as though she had known all along who was going to win. The waitress tripped over and said respectfully, "Another drink, sir?"

"The hell with it." I draped three bucks across the ash tray, stood up and crossed the floor. Once outside I turned and strolled down the narrow walk. No saps whistled through the air, no bullets ricocheted off the wall beside me. Just a calm tropic night with fragrance in the air and a lot of golden moon in the heavens. Perfection except for human beings who had to louse it up.

CHAPTER EIGHT

Somewhere up on the hill a band of colored boys were whaling the paint off their steel drums. The farther I walked toward the waterfront the fainter the music until at the water's edge it was only a drifting tinkle like muffled marimbas. The quiet bay was as dark as melted licorice. Moored along the promenade were luggers and ketches and fishing boats, their boom lanterns glowing orange and pale yellow like Hallowe'en window pumpkins. There were piles of cement bags, tiles, pipe and steel building rods, plumbing fixtures and lumber. In St. Thomas you imported everything except the sand.

A stern light showed gilt lettering across the transom of a white yawl: *Seabiscuit.* The boat that had brought Kelly back from Martinique. Near by a man was sitting on a mushroom bitt. Through the shadows I could see his white cap, white sneakers and the glow of his pipe. Captain Rip Andersen.

As I neared him he looked up, sucked noisily at his pipe and went back to staring out at the water. I said, "Quiet night, skipper."

"Yeah. This town's as lively as the storage vaults at Fort Knox."

"Depends on where you sit."

He shrugged. "I'm sittin' here. You see anything cheerful?"

I shook my head. "Two grand down the drain would make anyone sulky."

He spat into the water. "That's me."

I sat down on a near-by bitt, shook out a cigarette and lighted it. "Been working out of here long?"

"Long enough. Ever since the War."

"Navy?"

"Coast Guard. Sand Pounders they called us but I was a Beachmaster in the Solomons. I seen plenty sand pounded all right. By shells and bombs."

"Where you from?"

"Biloxi." He struck a match and sucked the flame into the pipe bowl. Then he flicked the match into the water. It made a tiny hiss. The steel band had stopped playing. From one of the luggers came the disconnected chant of a drowsy deckhand singing in Antilles patois. Otherwise everything was quiet. Andersen said, "Started out a shrimper. Easy work then—home every night. Then the damn War came along and I got patriotic—me and a couple million other guys. I got no gripe, though. Outside a couple shrapnel scars I scraped through lucky."

"Ever know Victor Polo?"

"I knew him the way I knew a lot of guys—knew him to wave to, to have a drink with. But I didn't gamble and don't."

"Except with charter customers."

"Yeah," he said sourly. "And this last one was a beaut. The bastard had the dough. He had to have it. If he didn't he wouldn't never got a girl like Kelly take a trip with him." He looked up at the star-spattered sky. "Whatta doll," he breathed.

"She's cruising under another registry now," I said. "Maybe you could get some dough out of her."

He moved his head slowly. "I thought of that, but what the hell, why make the kid miserable when it wasn't her fault? I got stuck and that's all there is to it. Next charter I'll get half in advance before I move a rope." He took the pipe out of his teeth, looked at the dead ashes and rapped them out against the side of the bitt. Then he stuck it in the pocket of his shirt and looked at me. "What makes you ask about a fellow like Victor Polo?"

"Curiosity, I guess."

"You a magazine writer? We get lots of magazine writers down here."

I shook my head. "Polo had to close up the Casino and get out of the islands. Not long afterward he was jailed for robbing a bank. Once out on parole he heads back here. Why? What did he leave in Saint Thomas that was worth coming back for?"

Andersen stretched his legs and jammed his hands in his pockets. "I heard a story about Polo once—a waterfront yarn, probably—but you're welcome to it." He cleared his throat. "Seems Polo and Dominic didn't get much notice before the Casino was raided. Just time enough to open their safe and split the cash on hand. Some say there was forty or fifty thousand dollars—others say twice as much." In the dimness I could see his white teeth exposed in a smile. He was enjoying the story.

"Well, there was all this hurry-up and confusion with the two partners splitting their dough and getting ready for the fast take-off. Bills all over the place. Dominic took charge of packing the cash into two bags—one for each of them. Dominic grabs his bag and heads for the hills—or maybe off to one of the French islands—until things quiet down. Polo grabs his bag and heads for Puerto Rico in a small boat. When he gets there—or maybe before—he opens his bag and damn near dies of heart failure."

"No green stuff," I said.

"Nothing greener than newsprint. Dominic pulled the gypsy switch on him and kept all the dough for himself."

"*Hokkano baro,*" I mused, "the Big Trick. The wallet switch done with suitcases."

"Yeah?" he sounded mildly interested. "After that I always figured Dominic for a gypsy—a Rumanian gypsy. Anyhow he was sharp enough to be one."

"So to get some dough Polo had to rob a bank. And he came back here finally to get what Dominic tricked him out of."

Andersen smiled. "*If* the tale's true."

"Where'd you hear it?"

"Hell, I heard it a dozen times. Always from Negro hands, now I think of it."

"And they could have heard it from the man who sailed Polo over to San Juan. Around here that kind of news would spread faster than the measles."

"How true. Seems I didn't get your name."

I told him and we shook hands. "I'd be glad to buy you a drink," I said.

"Hell, have one on me. I got plenty saved up from the guy who skipped ship in Martinique." He got up, stretched and we stepped across *Seabiscuit's* gunwale. Andersen ducked down the companionway and after a while he came up with ice, a seltzer bottle and a stone jug of scotch whisky. Thirty-year-old. The sight was enough to make a man slobber like a racehorse. Working the cork out of the jug, he hung it in the crook of his finger and poured it like cider. "Easy on the seltzer," I warned. "I wouldn't want to bruise the contents."

"Right. I figured you for a strong swimmer."

We were sitting in deck chairs, taking our ease and sipping antique grain slowly and appreciatively. After a while I said, "The tale you told me suggests that Dominic had a reasonable motive to want Polo out of the way. Any reason to think the police know the story?"

"Any reason to think they don't? This all happened a long time ago, remember. The police here are pretty smart boys. They'd naturally keep an eye on an ex-gambler like Dominic. If they ever heard he'd skinned Polo they'd remember it now that Polo's been killed." He tilted his glass and stared across the waterfront at the lights of Charlotte Amalie. "Looks a lot like Hong Kong," he mused. "At night Victoria Peak lights up like a big beautiful Christmas tree. Ever see it?"

"Once. After the Korean War."

"That was one I missed. What brings you down here?"

I told him. When he had heard me out he said, "Hope it goes through. The more tourists here the more charters for me." He lifted his glass. "Here's luck, Steve."

We drank and he refilled our glasses.

Through the still air, out of the waterfront darkness, came the sound of someone walking. Soles scuffing against the concrete surface. Not someone strolling along the promenade but someone cutting directly across it toward us. I sat up and listened.

Then out of the shadows came a woman. She walked to the side of the yawl and stepped across onto a transom. Andersen got up and said, "Welcome aboard, Kelly."

"Hi, Rip," she said and glanced at me. "Hello, Steve."

"Hello, Irish."

"What are you doing here—checking up on my past?"

I shook my head. "Way beyond that now. I was looking into your future."

"Were you?" she said petulantly. "And how do you find my chances?"

"A little under average." I put down my glass and pried myself up from the chair. "You've got business with the Captain, Irish. I'll shove along."

"That's not necessary. I'm not poisoning the air." She turned to Andersen. "I can give you some money now, Rip. Five hundred. Maybe I can get some more later on." She held out some folded bills.

Andersen said, "What'd you do, strike gold?"

I laughed shortly. "Even better than that. She met Simon Hargrave."

Her lips stiffened. "Take it, Rip."

He said, "Hell, Kelly, let it grow a while. I'm not exactly down to my last buck. Besides, you got passage back to the States to buy." He made no move to take the money from her hand.

I said, "Better grab it, skipper. The lady's of a changeable mind."

Kelly whirled. "You have no claim on me. I don't owe you a damn thing!"

I stepped toward the gunwale. "I kind of thought you did—after all the tender tears and quiet remorse. Anyway, don't give it a second thought now." I hooked my hand around a guy wire and pulled myself over onto the pier. " 'Night, folks." Turning, I began walking back toward town.

The moon was misty now, a silk-screen painting as fragile as a whisper in the dark. I pulled out a cigarette savagely and lighted it. Then I set my shoulders and lengthened my stride.

From the darkness behind me came running footsteps. Slowly I turned, then stopped. Kelly, of course. Her hair was flying behind her head and even in the darkness I could see moist silver on her cheeks. When she reached me she slowed, breasts heaving, and said, "Damn you, why'd you have to call me Irish?"

"It sort of came to me. Does what we call each other make any difference?"

"A boy called me that once. Years ago. He was my first sweetheart. No one ever called me Irish since—until tonight." Her fingers were brushing away the silver streaks. "I must be crazy letting it get me like this, letting it make a difference again." Her shoulders seemed to slump and the bravura left her voice. "I don't have to apologize to you for anything. You know that."

"I know that."

She shrugged. "I don't have to explain anything, either. Nothing."

"Nothing at all."

She looked at me bravely but her eyes were stippled with stars. "I'm sorry, Steve. Sorry for everything. Sorry about the trip and Rip and the marriage that didn't happen and coming back here and letting myself get sentimental over you. Christ, but I've made a mess of things."

"You've said that before."

One hand ran through her hair distractedly. "So I have. It's an old record now. Maybe I ought to change it."

I took out a cigarette and gave it to her. When I had lighted it, she said, "Rip wouldn't take the money. What do I do now?"

"Give it back to Hargrave. Or don't give it back to Hargrave. Use it for a trip to New York and a grubstake."

"It's only a loan," she said uncertainly. "Simon understands that."

"Sure he does. He'll have a lot of experience with long-term loans to lovely young ladies. He'll understand the principle as well as the dividends."

Her eyes narrowed. "You're a cold bastard," she breathed. "You don't give a girl anything, do you? Not even a thread of self-respect."

"It sort of depends on the girl. Have fun with Simon today?"

She shook her head shortly. "We were becalmed all afternoon. I thought we'd have to swim back."

"They carved that story inside the Pyramids."

She shrugged. "For some reason it's important to me that you believe there's nothing between us."

"There's half a G," I said, "and probably the promise of more. As much as you can stand."

"All right," she snapped. "The offer's there any time I want to accept it. Only so far I haven't decided. Any other comments?"

"Just one, Irish: millionaires don't drift past every day in the week so with this one I'd try to hold out for a ring."

Her hand flashed up and hit the side of my face smartly.

"He Who Gets Slapped," I said. "My day for Andreyev."

Suddenly she laughed. "Forgive me. Why are we standing here trading insults?"

"As if you didn't know."

Nodding slowly, she linked her arm through mine. "I guess one of the things I like about you is the way you insist on basics.

No pretense about you. In my phony world that's a startling contrast." She looked up at me. "Where were you going just now?"

"Anywhere, nowhere. I hadn't decided. I was still in a slow burn."

"From what?"

"From seeing you with Hargrave's money. He's tossing it around liberally today. Not an hour ago I could have had five grand from him."

"For what, Steve?"

"For very little. Leaving the Island."

"Why?"

"That's a good question. I had a couple of ideas and then I began to think he might feel more certain of you if I were out of the way. But that doesn't add up all the way, either. What's your guess?"

"I wouldn't have the foggiest."

We began walking slowly toward the edge of town. Her free hand brushed hair from her forehead and she said, "If you'd waited I'd have told you something that might interest you."

"Like what?"

"Like how the police came around to talk with Dominic just after sunset."

"That was to be expected."

"Sure. The police expected to find him, too. But they didn't."

I thought it over. Then I said, "He's gone? Really skipped?"

"Looks like."

"It's a small island," I said. "They'll find him. Unless he grabbed a boat the way Polo did."

"You think he went away because of Polo's murder?"

"That's what the police will think. Flight is considered tantamount to confession."

I felt her shiver against me. "God, what a creepy place, Steve. If I could get a plane out of here tonight, I would."

"There'll be one in the morning."

Her face turned and she said softly, "Maybe by morning I won't want to go. You said I had a changeable mind."

"There's that," I agreed and guided her toward the lights of Dominic's.

We went in by the back way and up dark stairs to her room. At the door I felt her press the key into my hand. Opening it, I stood aside to let her enter. Then I followed and closed the door behind me. She moved through the darkness and I heard the click of the bolt being shot. Throatily she said, "I could offer you a drink."

"I've had my limit."

"I could show you my stamp collection."

"That would mean turning on the lights."

"So it would," she said mock-seriously. "Any other suggestions, Steve?"

"Just this," I said, and found her with my arms.

For what seemed like a long time we kissed in silence. Then her thighs moved and sandals slapped against the wall. Barefoot she stood shorter than before. But not so short that her lips were beyond my reach. Her fingers were doing something with my hair, with the sensitive part of my ears. I felt her tongue glide tentatively between my lips. She shuddered then, broke away and in a moment I heard the soft swish of fabric dropping to the straw matting.

When she came back she crossed a thin shaft of moonlight. Against the darkness it dusted her naked body with silver.

CHAPTER NINE

When I woke it was long after three. I moved to the edge of the narrow bed and sat up. Then I leaned over and pulled the sheet across Kelly's shoulders. She moved in her sleep and buried her nose in the pillow. Like a child, I thought. I kissed the curve of her cheek and went away from the bed. Dressing in the darkness, I heard her quiet steady breathing. I tiptoed to the door, unbolted it quietly and slipped out into the hall. Kneeling in the darkness, I tied my shoelaces and stood up again. The band was no longer playing. There were no sounds from the direction of the bar. An early night at Dominic's. Maybe the crowd had heard the word and decided to stay away. I thought of Sybil Dominic and wondered if anyone had told her yet. In her case it would be kinder to wait until morning. I thought of Kelly and smiled happily. Then I began walking down the corridor.

A dim light at the end of the hall showed an oaken door lettered with the word: *Owner*. Dominic's room. I wondered what it would look like inside. Going quietly toward it, I listened for a moment and then I turned the knob and went in. As the door closed behind me a voice rasped, *"Hold it, you're covered."*

I froze.

A light flashed on and I blinked. The light glinted from the barrel of a revolver pointing at my stomach. The man who held it sat in a chair. A big man with sunburned hair, white ducks and a white shirt. "Oh, hell," he said sourly. "What's your story, Bentley?"

My friend from the Normandie Bar. The G-man. "Just curious," I said. "Believe it or not."

"Why should I believe it?"

"I care less than you could imagine," I said, reached slowly into my pocket and took out a cigarette. "I'd offer you one but you're on duty."

"Stake-out," he said sourly. "At my age. You had a brawl with Dominic today, beat him up pretty bad. He's missing now—as if you didn't know."

I lighted the cigarette, inhaled and leaned back against the door. "I heard the rumor going around."

"I'll just bet you did. So you got up at three-thirty in the morning, drifted down the hill and decided to check Dominic's bed. Why?"

"I wish I had a good answer for that one."

He looked down at the .38 Special and laid it along his thigh. He shifted his body as though it was cramped from sitting a long time. "I can't figure you out, Bentley. Coming here like this doesn't do you a damn bit of good with me. For your information the police have been looking for you. They'd like to know a little more about that fight with Dominic. The whys and wherefores."

"I had a witness."

He nodded. "We'd sort of like to hear a first-hand account."

"Making a Federal case out of a barroom brawl?"

"Maybe. There've been a couple of interesting developments since then. First, Dominic takes a powder. That's bad in itself—under the circumstances. Makes him look guiltier than a clerk with his hand in the till. Second, we find footprints leading down to the shore of an isolated beach over near Frenchtown. One set of footprints only, and none leading back." He sat forward and scratched the side of his face. "At the water's edge a pair of shoes and a pile of clothes. Whose clothes would they be?"

"Storm Dawn, the stripper's?"

"I wish they were. Ralph Dominic's. What would you make of all that?"

"Pretty obvious, no?"

"Plenty obvious. So obvious it could almost be window dressing."

"Any heel marks in the sand?"

He shook his head.

I said, "Holding down a joint like this is sweaty work. Maybe Dominic wanted a cool swim in the altogether before the evening lushes started pushing in."

"Possibly," he said, "but highly unlikely. Anything else?"

"Maybe he just got ashamed of the same old rags and wanted to dump them where the tide would get them."

"Very funny," he said mirthlessly.

"Well," I said, "I'm only trying to be helpful. Now the fact that you're sitting here means you expected someone to come through that door."

"Brilliant. Who did I expect to see?"

"Sonny Tyner," I ventured.

"No."

"Sybil Dominic?"

"Let's hope not. Nor her mother."

I gnawed my thumbnail. "Let's see, officer—could it—could it possibly be you expected to see the owner himself?"

"Positively a genius," he jeered.

"Then," I said, "you figure he hasn't left Saint Thomas yet."

"Where the hell could he go?"

"A strong swimmer could make it to Hassel Island and hide out like Robinson Crusoe. Or a boat could take him anywhere at all. Do you think Dominic killed Polo?"

"There's a motive." He raised one hand. "I'll take a cigarette."

I gave him one and lighted it. He sat back in his chair, yawned and said, "The Washington police think you're a grand fellow, Bentley. Or so a cable from Captain Kellaway tells me.

That's why you're not collared right now and sweating it out over at Fort Christian. On the other hand, this isn't the District of Columbia. It's my personal district and unlike the Washington police I'm not wild about amateur collaborators. So do me a favor and stay out of this. Have yourself a big time around this sun-kissed little resort and forget all about Victor Polo and Ralph Dominic."

"And Reba Royce?"

He shot me a sharp glance. "Her, too."

"Got that one figured out?"

"Maybe."

I knocked ash on Dominic's rug. Once it had been a clean rug but now it was streaked as though alcohol had spilled on it and dissolved the dye. A messed double bed and a breasty *Playboy* calendar on the wall. In one corner a desk littered with papers. An ash tray held the stub of a cigar. A wastebasket, shoes and swimming trunks. The room had a rank sweaty smell. It was Dominic's room all right. I wondered if Sybil had spent their married life in it.

"Well, no one's keeping you."

I turned and began to open the door.

"You'll remember what I said—about staying out of the case."

From the open doorway I said, "I'll remember. That doesn't mean I'll take the advice."

"I'm not kidding," he said heavily. "Drop it right here and now, Mr. Bentley. Down here you're up against heavyweights."

"My, my," I murmured, "such sterling advice so early in the morning. It takes a mighty clean-living fellow to be so alert so early in the day. And I've got ten bucks says nobody else comes here tonight."

"Just go," he said tiredly. "Give me that much of a break."

I closed the door and saw the strip of light under the door black out. Then I walked to the stairway and went down it and out into the back yard.

There wasn't much left of the moon. The wind from the sea was damp and cold. It held the taste of rain. I looked up at Kelly's dark window and then I walked to the alley and began trudging up the hill toward The Lodge.

Charlotte Amalie was asleep. Other than the sparse street lights only a few windows were lighted. There was a light over the post office door and one near the entrance of Fort Christian. I reached the parking area below the stairway to The Lodge and paused for breath.

The skin of the Volks was damp with dew. From somewhere came the heavy scent of jasmine, cloying and decadent. I ground my cigarette into the earth and got into the Volks. Turning on the radio, I listened to a San Juan disc jockey show for a while and then I turned it off. I was wide awake and restless. Releasing the Volks' brake I let it coast downhill, turned on the ignition and put in the clutch. The engine caught, backfired and held. I pointed the little car toward the waterfront and turned west.

Along the pier the moored boats rocked quietly. They were dark and lifeless, ghost ships in the night. A cloud gnawed at the edge of the moon. Here beside the water the air was colder than on the hill; damper and scented with decay. I thought of the good burghers of Charlotte Amalie tucked securely in their legal beds. I thought of Mrs. Vane Drury snoring heavily in her alcoholic slumber; I thought of Sybil stirring in her troubled dreams and then I thought again of Kelly, her snub nose pushed into the pillow, the graceful curve of her shoulder and the litheness of her naked arm. It was the only image that gave me any comfort.

The dark road was deserted. I was outside town now, and passing the old French cemetery. But for the clouded moon I could have seen the old gravestones, the tottering fence, the whitewashed monuments and the gnarled sapodilla trees. I was glad the cloud hid all that.

Bouncing over the lane between the Cha-Cha sheds, into the clearing and past the dark Normandie Bar, and around behind it to the point of land where the old Casino stood. The moon came from behind a cloud and showed it starkly against the darker background. A ghost house. A house to be filled with bats and flickering lights. Steady, Bentley, don't let it get you. Only an old empty house and no one believes in ghosts. No? Then what of hate and love? If love lives after death then what of hate? If love can fill a house why not hate as well? Hate and fear. Shivering a little I turned off the ignition and flicked off the headlights.

Around me nothing but heavy silence. Not even the chirp of a tree frog or a lizard. No scary flutter of bat wings either for that matter. Reaching into the glove compartment, I took out a trouble flashlight and pulled off the red plastic lens. I tried the light in my cupped hand. The batteries were good.

I slid quietly out of the Volks, wondering what the hell difference it made after having driven up with my headlights on. There was sand underfoot and spidery patches of crabgrass. In all of Frenchtown not a light to be seen. Beyond the docks I could make out the brooding bulk of Hassel Island, but that was all. No friendly lights in fishing boats. No fishing boats at all. I was alone.

Setting my teeth, I began walking toward the Casino porch.

I was halfway there when my foot caught under a strand of crabgrass, nearly tripping me. Straightening, I felt sweat on my forehead. I wiped it off on my forearm and it was cold. In the shadows of the porch I could barely see the front door. I knew it was nailed shut. To enter that way I would need a crowbar. A better time to break in would be by daylight, but someone would notice me then.

At the corner of the porch I paused and scanned the length of the building. Farther along there was another door and a row of windows. I was in the middle of a step when my eyes made out something on the porch boards. Something that made my breath stop in my throat.

I saw a hat and a pair of shoes and a body stretched between. A man's body. Gripping the flashlight, I moved toward it.

Two yards away I made out a man's hand. The hand rested on the throat of a guitar. The man was lying on his back. Suddenly he snored. The harsh sound nearly made me jump. I swore softly and turned away. Old Henry again. An old wreck sleeping in a ruin. Taking a deep breath, I felt my pulse slow and then I continued slowly around the side of the house.

The first two windows were locked. I tried the door and shone the flashlight through the glass. Inside it was braced shut by a two-by-four. Swearing, I moved on to the third window. Near the catch a pane of glass was missing. I reached in and tried to move it but it was rusted tight. The butt of my flashlight nudged it free, shrieking like a dying cat as it came open.

I was concentrating on the work and sweating a little. The position was awkward, leaning forward and stretching upward and twisting and prying all at the same time. Even if I had been listening for it I couldn't have heard a stealthy footstep in the cushioning sand. All that I heard was a soft *whish* somewhere above me like the tail of a shooting star. My body tensed and my head jerked up but I was too late. Much too late. Something with the heft of a steel girder crashed into the back of my head and I fell forward against the house. My fingers clawed the clapboards uselessly, then strength snapped away like a cut elastic band. My world became a universe of whirling color and unbearable pain. Suddenly it shattered like a frozen globe and the fragments flew away, leaving me in utter darkness.

CHAPTER TEN

It was a soft, crooning sound. Remote and impersonal as a ventriloquist in a vacant hall. It dropped to a low chuckling and I felt something plucking at my arm, something trying to move me. I groaned and rolled away. The chuckling sound stopped.

Opening my eyes, I saw gray sand. I lifted my head and stared at crabgrass under the swaying spears of a low palmetto. Turning painfully, I blinked at the knees of a man crouched beside me. His patched trousers were faded with age. He wore a red, red shirt, a Cha-Cha hat and a silvery growth of whiskers. A black man with leathery fingers that twitched. Old Henry. Elbowing myself up, I closed my eyes in pain and touched the back of my head. It felt bigger than a ripe muskmelon. My fingers found a long dry crust matted in my hair. Wincing, I opened my eyes again and looked at Henry. My wallet was half out of my inside pocket. I pushed it back where it belonged and snarled, "Corpse robber."

Henry gazed at me unimpressed.

I said, "I didn't think you had the strength."

Lips drew back over teeth whiter than bleached ivory. "I didn't drop you, mon. I only jus' foun' you."

"When?"

"Now, mon. Jus' now."

I glanced at my wristwatch. Nearly five-thirty. I had taken a long dive. A long steep dive into deep dark water. The way my head felt I was lucky to have drifted back to the surface. "Who socked me?" I croaked.

His hands spread in an elemental gesture of ignorance.

"Great," I said. "If you didn't, Henry, who did? Who else comes around here at night?"

His lips parted again. He half-hummed, half-chanted, *"Mistah Victah Polo was a money mon...."*

"Polo's dead," I snapped. "I've been slugged by live men before but never by a ghost. And I don't dig voodoo." Shakily I began to get up. Gradually and by degrees. Henry stopped chanting and watched me stolidly. Pulling a dollar bill from my pocket, I dropped it on his knees. "This is for forgetting I came here. Anytime you hear who dropped me there's five more waiting for you."

Skinny fingers crumpled the bill. It disappeared inside the pocket of his blood red shirt.

No sun yet. Just hazy gray sky and a dull pewter sea. The air was cold and damp. Like air in a granite mausoleum. My clothes were wet with dew. Henry got up and walked toward the front porch. Leaning forward, he picked up his guitar, whanged an open-string chord and adjusted his frayed Cha-Cha hat. Then he began shuffling away. I watched him go. A wired skeleton had more meat on it than Henry. I felt dizzily sick and groped for the side of the building. My flashlight lay in the sand. When my stomach calmed down I leaned over slowly and picked it up. A hell of a lot of good it had done me.

There were marks in the sand, anonymous impressions that could have been footprints. But their trail led nowhere, told no story at all. I sucked in a deep painful breath and began walking back to where I had left the Volks. It was still there, stippled with dew, key in the ignition lock. Lowering myself slowly into the seat, I rested a moment and turned on the ignition. The engine was cold but I nursed it along and finally it caught and held. Slowly I backed the bug around and found the sandy trail. Henry was trudging over toward the Normandie Bar. There was a light inside. My dollar was good for at least four drinks. That should set Henry up for half a day. Unless Big John slapped him down.

I drove across the open area in front of the Normandie and turned through the Cha-Cha sheds. Board window shutters were propped open and an old woman was starting a backyard fire under a rusty laundry tub. Sitting on the block steps of a Cha-Cha shack was Pierre Duroc. He had a short cigarette in his mouth and a thick coffee cup in one hand. The gray baseball cap was perched on the back of his head. He saw me drive past and watched me with uncommunicative eyes. I wondered if Pierre had snuck up behind me and slammed a sap against my skull. Why not? Pierre or anyone else could have done it. The question was why.

As I turned onto Harwood Highway, I saw two Cha-Chas trundling a wheelbarrow into the overgrown old cemetery. The barrow held two long-handled shovels suitable for grave-digging. Preparing the ground for Victor Polo. In life you thought you needed a lot of things: money, possessions and acres of land. And at the end all you really needed was a six-by-two plot wherever you happened to fall. Nausea swelled over me again and I gripped the wheel hard. When the wave receded I propped my eyes open, gritted my teeth and drove into Charlotte Amalie.

The stone steps to The Lodge were steeper and longer than ever. Halfway up I sat down and put my face in my hands. I felt as though I had battled a cageful of polar bears and lost. After a while I got up, hooked one hand around the iron rail and pulled myself the rest of the way.

Through the shutters of my room I could see the sun's orange arc rising from the edge of the sea. The air was still in the peculiar quiet of dawn on the water. No insects, no birds, no lugger sails, no drifting clouds. Nothing moving. For a brief instant I had the crazy feeling that everyone else had ceased to exist and I was the only living thing on the Island.

Stripping to my shorts, I lay down on the bed. Not much later I decided it had been a poor idea to turn in without some pain-killer so I rummaged in my shaving kit for the aspirin bottle, swallowed four jumbo tablets and sacked out again. After a while the pain ebbed away and I slept.

The room was hot when I woke. Flies buzzed on the ceiling. I raised myself stiffly and blinked at my watch. Nearly noon. Groping into the bathroom I stared at eyes redder than peeled grapes stuck in a tallowy, unshaven face. It was enough to make even a strong man retch. I felt weak and played out. Even shaving was a major effort.

I poured ice water from the thermos jug, swallowed another brace of aspirin, dressed and went groggily down the stairway to the veranda.

Sonny was sitting on a bench reading the morning paper. He looked up and said, "You've developed Island habits without much trouble."

"I'm not a well man," I said, sinking into a chair. "Not well at all."

A frown flickered across his face. "What's wrong, Steve?"

I told him.

While he was listening he put aside the paper. Then he got up, mixed two stiff highballs and carried them back. "Under ordinary circumstances, I wouldn't recommend this."

"Under routine conditions I wouldn't take it." Tilting the glass, I let the cold whisky slide down my raw gullet. Then I shook myself like a spaniel coming out of an icy pond. "What's so special about the old Casino I get slugged for prowling around it?"

He lighted a cigarette, put away the gold lighter and said, "What's so special about the old Casino you had to go prowling?"

"Hell, I had half an idea Dominic might be holed up there."

"You need food, Steve."

"That and kind words," I said. "Why did Hargrave offer me five grand to go away from here?"

He stared at me and tugged the lobe of one ear.

"You having trouble with him over the Coco Isle business?"

"None I know of. It's obvious Simon didn't like you. I couldn't figure out why not. I still can't."

I waved one hand. "Vibrations, maybe. Or oil and water. Anyway, we're incompatible. There's a lot of your money tied up in this thing. I wouldn't want to sour the deal for you."

"I can handle Simon. Don't worry about it." He got up, walked off toward the kitchen and called the maid. I heard him ordering breakfast for me and then he came back. He was wearing tan leather *chaplis* on his feet, black linen shorts and a madras sport shirt. Very cool and classier than an ad for Puerto Rican rum. I said, "If that's the case, let's get down to business today."

He frowned. "I forgot to mention the police want to talk to you. About your fight with Dominic."

"The hell with them."

"I'll go down with you if you want."

"At the moment I can't think of anything less inviting. How are things with Allegra?"

"Tolerable. I think she'll stick with me. I want her to, God knows."

I lighted a cigarette and inhaled. The smoke was drier than cement dust. What the hell did I expect? Caramel flavoring? "Two murders and a disappearance that may be death, suicide or murder," I mused. "And the only clues a couple of bundles of old clothes. If a man's going to drown himself he doesn't strip first, he wades on in knowing the added weight will drag him down faster. Leaving Polo out of it for the moment, the fact that we found Dominic's clothes suggests he was planning a reasonably long swim and didn't want to be hampered by clothes. Why? I don't get it."

His face darkened. "The son of a bitch killed Reba, that's why. He was making his getaway."

"Where could he swim to from that beach? Hassel Island if he had good wind. There or some other point of land. But until he's found, the presumption has to be he didn't make it."

"That's what Vane's presuming. She's happier than a cricket."

"Tell her to take it easy on that barnyard crowing," I said. "That girl of hers is half-hysteric already. It wouldn't take much of a shove to push her the rest of the way."

He nodded thoughtfully. The maid came in with a tray, lowered it and went away. The waffles were crisp and golden, the maple syrup came from Vermont and when I had downed a second cup of creamy coffee I felt I could stand on my feet without shaking. That soon, it seemed a major victory.

The maid took away the tray and I heard the scrape of shoes on the stairway. I saw Hargrave's head first, then Vane Drury.

Vane was zanily cordial and Hargrave acknowledged me briefly. Sonny ducked into his office, brought out the working papers and began to discuss them. My head still throbbed and I found it hard to concentrate. Once I caught Hargrave regarding me with what could have been the beginning of a sardonic grin. Then his mouth straightened and he glanced away. I wondered if he was the son of a bitch who had cold-calked me eight hours before.

There wasn't much for me to do but sit there and listen to the partners argue about their corporation. A few drinks made everyone mellow—everyone but me—and by two o'clock general agreement had been reached. To keep the corporation in the family they decided that in the event of the death of one partner his shares would be divided evenly between the surviving two. Vane had wanted her shares to go to Sybil but she was outvoted. And so it stayed.

When they left, Sonny reminded me about the police so we walked down the stairway and into the dank coolness of old Fort Christian.

It didn't take as long as I thought it would. They listened with mild interest to my description of the fight, thanked me and asked me not to leave the Island without telling them. As we walked back into the sunlit street I wondered if my big friend was still sitting up in Dominic's room or whether he had given up, finally, and turned in. He should have gone with me last night where the hunting was better. Better for someone. Every time I remembered being slugged I got a little madder. I didn't think Dominic had done it because I was still alive. Dominic would have put his foot on my throat and stamped on it until I stopped jerking. My lips were dry. I licked them and decided I needed another drink. What I really needed was a plane seat hack to Washington but I was in it too far to pull out now. I had to stay and see it through.

Sonny said, "Siesta time, Steve. You look pretty frayed."

"I feel even worse," I said. "Trouble is if I lie down I'm afraid I might not get up again. I'm that rocky."

He shrugged. "Don't try to do too much. This sun is a killer." He looked at me. "You're going to keep poking around, looking for trouble?"

"Poking around, anyway."

"Trouble found you last night. I wouldn't challenge it again."

"Nature of the beast," I sighed. "Anyway, thanks for standing by me during the grilling."

"Hell, that was nothing. I wish all they had against me was slugging Dominic."

"Maybe I'll take a tourist spin in a glass-bottom boat and peer at the undersea gardens."

"The hell you will."

"Or I could drive Kelly Martin up to Bluebeard's Castle for lunch and a lazy afternoon."

"That's more like it." He grinned and started walking back up the hill. I veered into a sidewalk liquor store, bought a pint of wheat in a plain wrapper and carried it up to where I had parked the Volks. The windows were down so the air inside was breathable. Un-braking the little car, I let it coast down the hill, starting the engine near the bottom. From there I headed toward the waterfront and Dominic's seaside saloon.

It hadn't changed since yesterday. The outside gave no clue to the absence of the owner. Or to the murder of its star dancer for that matter. I nosed the Volks into the shadow of a big forsythia bush and trudged around to the back stairs. Knocking at Kelly's door, I took out a cigarette and waited. No answer. "Rise and shine, Irish," I called. Still no answer. I tried the door but it was locked. Lighting my cigarette, I walked down the corridor past Dominic's quarters and emerged in the barroom.

Miscellaneous couples were drinking their lunch along the seaside railing. Behind the bar the bartender nodded in the drowsy heat. I hooked my heels on a stool and requested scotch on the rocks. He came awake then, blinked and scooped ice chips into a glass. The drink he poured me was darker than Honduran mahogany.

Taking the glass from him, I said, "If the boss was around you'd never get away with pouring a drink like this."

He smiled. "Boss ain't around. Guess I'm runnin' the place till he comes back. I kind of like it this way."

"What happened to Miss Martin?"

"Gone out."

"Alone?"

"Mistah Simon Hargrave come by a while back. They drove off somewhere."

The scotch in my mouth turned as bitter as green grapefruit. I set down my glass and stared out over the harbor. There were little whitecaps on the water. It would be a better day for sailing than yesterday; maybe they wouldn't be becalmed again. I thought about Kelly, remembering last night, and then I thought about Hargrave. Hell, I couldn't blame her. Her film career was shot. If she went back to New York she'd be one of a thousand chic models fighting for assignments but with no chance for a cover spread because her face was too well known. The model mills used new faces, fresh faces. Two seasons and a girl was lucky if she could pose for an overshoe catalogue.

A car bounced in from the road and headed for the parking area outside. A Hillman convertible, Sybil's car. She wore large dark glasses and her hair was bound up in a batik turban. Before the dust settled she was out of the car and walking purposefully toward the door. The bartender saw her and moved toward the end of the bar. She didn't notice me. Her hands gripped the edge of the bar and she said something to the bartender. He shook his head regretfully and she bit her lip. Her shoulders seemed to slump and I thought she was going to cry. Instead her head turned and she saw me. She left the bartender and came toward me.

"Hello, Steve," she said huskily. "You know about Ralph, don't you?"

I nodded.

"Do you think he's dead?" she asked tightly. "Everyone else does."

"Not everyone. There's some opinion holds he's only lying low until things quiet down."

"What things?"

"Polo's murder—and Reba's."

She tossed her head impatiently. "Ralph had nothing to do with them."

"Then I wouldn't worry about him. If he's alive he'll come back. He's got money tied up in this place. He wouldn't check out without cashing it in."

Her head lowered. "Jesus, I feel lousy."

"That makes two of us. Let's get sobbing drunk."

She smiled faintly. "That could be easier than you'd imagine." She got onto the stool beside me. For the first time I noticed her wedding ring. A thin gold band. No engagement ring. Dominic wouldn't have bothered with sentimental nonsense.

"Rum on the rocks," she told the bartender and turned to me. "What's wrong with you today?"

"A man trotted off with my girl."

Her eyebrows knitted. "I didn't know you had a girl."

"She's anybody's girl. Anybody who can offer her a future."

"You blame her for that?"

"I'm not even going to try."

She lifted her glass. "Cheers, Steve."

"Yeah." We drank together.

When she lowered her glass she inspected the back of my head. "You're a mess. How'd you get that?"

I told her. When I had finished, her lips tightened and she turned away. Quietly she said, "You think Ralph's a murderer, don't you?"

"I think it's possible."

"I don't."

"You're probably a minority of one. Why did Victor Polo come back here, Sybil?"

Her lips closed firmly and she shook her head.

I said, "Was it to retrieve the money Dominic bilked him out of when the Casino closed down?"

Her eyes widened. "You've heard that story, too."

"Many people have. Including the police. If it's true it makes almost a prima facie case against Dominic."

"I'll give him an alibi," she said. "I'll swear he stayed with me all that night."

"Wives are the worst possible witness for their husbands. Everyone knows the two of you were separated, that he couldn't stand the sight of you."

Her face was gaunt, her cheeks hollow. "Don't say that," she said harshly.

"Anyway, I wouldn't build that alibi thing any bigger. It's a natural impulse but a poor one."

"God, you're cynical."

"The way of the world," I said airily.

Picking up her glass, she drained it and put it down on the bar. Then she slid off the stool and stared at me, "I've got to find Ralph. The longer he stays away the worse it looks for him. I know he didn't kill Polo or Reba. He's got to come back now and prove it." She turned and walked quickly out of the bar.

Pulling out a dollar bill, I handed it to the bartender. "When the redhead comes back—assuming she comes back—tell her the backstairs boy friend was looking for her."

He smiled understandingly. "Anything else?"

"Nothing comes to mind." I got off the stool, went back through the corridor and noticed that Dominic's door had been wired shut with a lead seal. Interesting, if I had time to think about it. As I went down the stairs I heard the Hillman driving away.

I got into the Volks, started it and edged ahead until I could see Sybil driving west along the waterfront. Then I put the car into gear, drove out to the promenade and followed.

CHAPTER ELEVEN

Sybil Dominic drove rapidly, skittering around donkey carts and natives with market baskets balanced on their heads. At the end of the promenade she veered inland and I lost sight of her behind a row of houses. On Harwood Highway I spotted her again heading toward Frenchtown. Beyond the cemetery she turned in.

As I drove past marble city, someone was being buried. A priest stood at the head of a newly dug grave. On a near-by donkey cart lay a wooden coffin. The gravediggers were leaning on their shovels. There were maybe a dozen people standing around the grave, colored mostly, with four or five curious Cha-Chas. And one uniformed policeman. About right for Victor Polo's requiem.

By the time I reached the clearing the Hillman was nowhere to be seen, but I hadn't expected Sybil to be guzzling at the Normandie Bar. Parking in the shade of the building, I got out of the Volks and began hiking toward the Casino. Fresh wheel grooves in the sandy lane told me my hunch was right.

Keeping close to the bordering foliage, I heard a car engine shut off and when I reached the edge of what had been the Casino lawn I saw Sybil moving carefully across the boards of the front porch. Her fists hammered the door and I heard her call Dominic's name. Her voice was threaded with despair. I felt grubby suddenly, a shabby eavesdropper, a listener on a private line. Sybil stepped back from the door, turned and went quickly down the steps and around the far side of the big rotting house. I moved through the underbrush and stopped behind a palmetto where I could see the window I had tried to enter last night. The place where I had been slugged.

From the side of the house came Sybil's call again, as forlorn as a lost seabird. I wondered if anyone would answer.

Then from the foliage twenty yards away someone stepped into the clearing. Not Rima the Jungle Girl but a man. He was wearing chino pants, a faded Army shirt and his right hand held a Colt .45. A short, heavily built man with bulldozer shoulders. He could have been Dominic, but the gray baseball cap told me differently.

Pierre Duroc stood listening, head cocked to one side, the pistol dangling at the end of his right arm. Above him a jungle bird gave a harsh cry, swooped from a high branch and landed on another. Pierre looked up quickly, then went back to listening. Just then Sybil's calling stopped. I felt hair along my spine start to prickle.

But in a moment she came half-running around the far side and got into the Hillman. She started the engine and slammed the car into gear. The wheels spun in the sand, caught and she backed around. By now Pierre was back in his hiding place. Before the Hillman passed me, I ducked down and saw it go by, spraying sand, slewing along the rutted lane until it was out of sight. I stayed where I was until my knees began to ache. Then I straightened slowly. Pierre moved into the clearing again and this time the pistol was in his belt. Standing with his hands on his hips, he surveyed the Casino. Then he began walking toward it. As quietly as I could, I followed.

Pierre reached the window I had almost succeeded in opening and stared at it. He fitted his fingertips into the crevice and pried upward but the latch held; I hadn't quite freed it. Then he bent over and began scanning the sand.

From ten feet away I called, "Looking for buried treasure?"

He spun around wildly and his right hand went for the butt of his gun. His cheeks were streaked with white. Then he saw me, shrugged and his hand dropped away. He forced a tight laugh. As I neared him he said, "Someone come here last night."

"I know. Someone else came here. You?"

"Why would I come here?" He lifted his cap casually, scratched the top of his head and replaced it. His face was as gray as his cap.

"Why would anyone come here? With or without a gun?"

His eyes flickered to the Colt in his belt, then to mine. He shrugged and a foolish look grew and covered his face. He was going into the slob act again. It was almost believable.

"Mon's got a right to protect himself," he said with an ingratiating smile.

I shook out a cigarette, lighted it and inhaled deeply. "How would you know anyone came here last night—unless you were here, too?"

"Henry say so. He tell many people."

"Look, Pierre," I said, "if I had even half a notion you sapped me last night I'd swipe your baseball cap and bloody your nose. What saves you is that old Henry just possibly could have run off at the mouth. Drunks have been known to do that."

His mouth twisted unpleasantly. "You're not so big."

"I'm big enough," I said, "and I haven't got a malt paunch either. You hear someone was here last night so you start nosing around. I'd be interested in knowing why."

His grin was sly and foolish, almost servile. He hooked his thumbs in his belt and seemed to relax. "Someone's been stealin' Pa's nets at night. I figured maybe I could catch the guy."

I laughed shortly. "Your pa's nets get stolen at night so you hang around here in the daytime. That makes less sense than stalking deer with a calliope. Now, the other thing I don't like is the careful attention Mrs. Dominic just got from you. Why didn't you step out and make yourself known, offer to give her a hand?"

"Why didn't you?" he sneered.

His feet were planted solidly. His shoulders had lifted slightly, aggressively. From his belt the blue steel gunmetal gave off a glow as cold as frozen flint. If I was going to mix it with Pierre I would pick another time and place. And a better reason.

For a full minute we eyed each other like hostile dogs and then his eyes broke it off. His shoulders relaxed and he idled toward me. "Hell," he muttered, "no reason to make a big thing out of it. I'm Cha-Cha French. Cha-Chas don't like strangers hanging around Frenchtown."

"Is Dominic alive or dead?"

His smile was loose-lipped. Like a feeblo. "Who knows?"

I said, "I came here last night thinking this would be a pretty fine place to hole up if a man wanted to stay out of sight. Have you been inside lately?"

He spat on the sand. "This morning. Soon as I saw you drive away. Nothing there. I had the same idea."

I fished the pack of cigarettes from my pocket and he took one and lighted it. Tension had drifted away and I began to get the idea that Pierre might be halfway legitimate. And for a Cha-Cha that was giving him a lot. He was smart, too, or shrewd; more probably the latter. But if he'd checked the Casino earlier why had he tried to pry the window open just now?

Smoke idled from his nostrils. He said, "Hot today. Think I'll maybe go swimming."

"I've heard worse ideas."

Nodding, he stepped past me and took the path back toward the Normandie Bar. I let him get ten yards ahead of me and then I followed.

Pierre crossed the clearing and drifted into the bar. Old Henry was sitting on the ground in the shade, his back propped against the side of the building. His guitar lay across his thighs and he was asleep. By now the dollar bill was long gone. Looking at him reminded me of last night's cosh job and I got mad all over again. Pierre's .45 could have been the instrument, that or anything else. I touched the back of my head gingerly and slid into the Volks.

By the time I drove past the cemetery the grave-diggers were shoveling sandy soil into the narrow pit. Another two feet and the grave would be filled. The donkey cart was gone and so were the hangers-on and the priest. A lonely grave. I wondered if Victor Polo had been a pimp as well as a gambler; how many Island girls he had shipped down the line to Manaos and São Paulo and Porto Alegre. It was a secret between him and the walls of his board coffin.

Before turning onto Harwood Highway I unscrewed the top of the pint bottle and let an ounce trickle between my lips. It burned my throat like vitriol and pain leaped high in my head, crashing into the top of my skull. Then the pain subsided and a glow of well-being began to seep outward from the pit of my stomach. I coughed a couple of times and put the bottle away. An odd, offbeat character, Pierre Duroc. Twice I had found him lurking around Victor Polo's old Casino. And two days before it had been his pa who had found Polo's body drifting in the water. That gave the Duroc family, *père et fils,* a near monopoly of Polo's affairs.

As the Volks idled over the blacktop road I wondered what Polo's movements had been between the time he reached St. Thomas and his death; who had he seen, what had he done. That was police work, though. The police would know the hour of his arrival, what taxi he had taken to his hotel and at what hotel he had registered. The police would be able to quiz the clerk and the bartender and the dining-room help to establish Polo's contacts. There seemed to be nothing in that for me.

An old sedan bore down on me and I recognized Big John's taxi. He had a load of passengers and he was heading for the airport as though the plane were halfway off the strip. If he blew a tire at that speed he would end up in the ditch. That would be troublesome to most men but not to big John. He could yank a taxi out of a ditch without working up a good sweat. All that on a diet of fried bananas, fried fish and whisky. It seemed a lot for a little. I should try it sometime. I should try it from now on in.

The Volks was only making about twenty-five and a small car pulled around and passed me. It was a Hillman convertible with the top down and the driver was Sybil Dominic. Her face was calm and she sat back against the seat in a relaxed, easy way. Glancing at me, her eyebrows lifted in recognition and she waved at me cheerfully. This was a different Sybil Dominic than the taut girl in the barroom, a different Sybil than the one who had called so wildly for Dominic around the Casino. Then the Hillman drew ahead and widened the distance between us. The thought was worth a shrug and nothing more.

A scrawny dog ran across the road and I swerved in time to spare its mangy hide. It would be struck down another time, at some predetermined hour and moment. Death speaks: We were all an *Appointment in Samarra* generation. A yellow-breasted bird darted low over the road, followed by its mate. Above, not a cloud in the sky. In the harbor a big three-masted schooner slid past Hassel Island, looking like a pirate brig from an old Tyrone Power swashbuckler.

Up at The Lodge there was work I could do. Now that the partners had reached agreement I could finish what I had come to St. Thomas to do and get back to Washington with my fee and an aching head.

Inland, a hundred yards away, stood Dominic's saloon. I stared at it remembering the sensual, insinuating dance of Reba Royce. The ad sign was still there, no one had bothered to change it: *Reba Royce and Her Bamboushay Calypsos Nightly from Nine O'Clock*. A tantalizing jungle girl, a covert plaything of men ashamed to acknowledge desire for a mulata. A fragment of bawdy verse flashed through my mind: *The blacker the berry the sweeter the juice; Ah keeps a nigrah for mah pussonal use....*" Shag her down in the cornfield, son, but don't let white Missy catch you at it.

Where *Seabiscuit* had been moored the pier was vacant. Cap'n Rip Andersen had shoved off or moved to another mooring. I liked the way he had turned down Kelly's money and I wished him luck.

Turning off the promenade, I saw the untidy figure of Vane Drury leaving the courthouse steps. She crossed the square and pushed through swinging doors into the alcoholic cavern where I had spent part of last evening—the better part as I remembered it.

On the far side of the square I found a yard of shade and parked the Volks. Entering the bar I found myself in almost total darkness. Mrs. Drury was sitting at the bar, guzzling a long drink. When she saw me she nodded and indicated a stool beside hers. I slung myself onto it and she said, "Buy you a drink, Steve."

Her words were fuzzy. The drink in her hand was by no means the first since lunch. The blond bartender took my order.

"Just been to the courthouse," Vane slurred. "Everything's goin' jus' fine. Jus' fine, Steve." She whalloped me across the back.

I coughed, grimaced and said, "That pleasures me mightily."

"Thank you," she said with alcoholic gravity. "Thank you ver' much. Ver' much, indeed."

I said, "Seems sort of pointless to go on with the divorce when Sybil's probably a widow right now."

Her eyes narrowed. "Better make sure than sorry."

The blond bartender put down my drink in front of me. In the blue light her lined face looked like a cracked mirror. She smiled engagingly, lighted a cigarette and leaned back against the bottle shelf. She kept on watching me.

Vane tapped my shoulder. "Now Dominic's gone I c'n tell you something, Stevie." She rolled the words in her mouth, savoring them like peppermint drops. I gave her my polite attention.

She gave me a lopsided grin. "Don' make many mistakes, Stevie, but when I make one, bet your rump it's a beaut." She shook her head and chuckled softly, boozily. Lifting her glass, she guzzled more liquor she didn't need and said, "Made a big mistake once. Thought I'd do the right thing by Dominic—before he got to treating my Sybil bad. I gave him my interest in Coco Isle."

I stared at her. "That *is* interesting," I said. "What did you do that for?"

She waved a hand as though to clear away smoke I couldn't see. "Taxes, Stevie. You oughta know that. Death taxes, inheritance taxes. I wanted them to have as much of it as the law allowed. So I assigned my share to Ralph Dominic." She made a sour face. "Damn fool thing to do. Best intentions in the world. Then they broke up. Dominic had the paper." She gave me a bleary smile. "Sybil's his widow now, so it's all hers the way it oughta be."

I lifted my glass and sipped slowly. The blond bartender had a bony chest. The orange-colored tulle didn't do anything for her either. I could visualize her build: legs as skinny as gas pipes and slightly bowed; flat bony buttocks and a serpentine spine prone to arthritis in later years. Weight about ninety pounds in her shoes, falsies and nylons. Not much to roll against in a double bed.

I tried to get my mind back on the track. I wasn't concentrating too well. Scotch with ice and rum with ice and outside heat and then scotch without ice and now the drink in my hand. All that on top of a sap-addled head. Not too smart, Bentley. Tropical heat squeezes a man so dry he spends the rest of his days soaking up moisture in humid bars.

I blinked and put down my glass. The bartendress was frowning at me. She must have read my thoughts telepathically. She had a right to pummel my cheeks if she wanted to. I looked at Vane Drury and said, "Good for you. In skeet parlance, a double."

She nodded drowsily. "Deserve some luck. Deserve to see Sybil married to someone right for her." Her eyelids lifted slyly.

"You look about right, Stevie. Gentleman. Polite. Not a catter, not a boozer. You married or not? I disremember."

"Not that I know of."

Her fingers tapped my arm. "Like you," she confided. "Sensible young man. Sybil's rich young widow now. Think about it."

The bartendress uttered a laugh like the caw of a robber crow. Turning, she splashed scotch into a shot glass and tossed it off.

The swinging doors opened, a shaft of sunlight spotted the dark floor and Allegra Tyner came in. Her hands were small fists as she peered blindly into the darkness. Then she took three short steps forward and called, "Steve, come with me. Right away." Her voice rose, teetered on a false note and broke.

I got down off the stool. "Sure," I said. "What's happened?"

"Sonny," she said unsteadily. "They've taken him to jail, Steve. They're charging him with murdering Reba Royce."

CHAPTER TWELVE

They were booking Sonny when we got to Fort Christian. The lawyer was a slight, bald-headed man with thin lips and an undertaker's approach to life. No bail, he informed us, and Sonny would be transferred to San Juan tomorrow. "Change of venue," he explained. "Under the circumstances it seemed a wise thing to request."

"Under what circumstances, Mr. Meadows?"

"Why, the racial angle. Look at the racial proportions here, Mr. Bentley," he sniffed. "That ought to suggest the reason to you."

Allegra stared dully at her hands. "I guess it's the thing to do," she said finally. "I'll go to San Juan, of course."

I said, "What evidence are they charging him on?"

"A prima facie case, they say. That's all I've been able to get from them. We'll hear the rest in court."

"That's telling us a hell of a lot," I grated and saw my white duck amigo come out of a room. There was a policeman talking with him. To Meadows I said, "I think you'd be a lot smarter to start throwing bricks in the fan. Get a writ of habeas corpus, challenge the jurisdiction. Do anything. I'm just about certain Sonny didn't kill Reba Royce, but if he's cleared in San Juan the muttering in these Islands will never end. He's no tourist. Meadows, he lives here. He's brought money into the Islands, provided jobs. If a jury finds him guilty, let it be here. If they find him innocent, let it be here, too."

Meadows's lip stiffened. "Mrs. Tyner," he said, "there can be only one legal tactician in this case. Either my advice is followed or I beg to withdraw."

"Sold." I stared coldly at him.

Allegra said, "I ... I don't know what to say. I just want what's best for Sonny."

I said, "In any case, Meadows, you won't be pleading the case—if it ever gets to trial. We'll bring some real legal talent down here. I'll bet you haven't tried a criminal case for twenty years."

His face got dangerously red. "Mrs. Tyner," he spluttered, "I find this man's interference and imputations intolerably objectionable. I must insist that—"

"Quite a mouthful, Counselor," I cut in. "Now we'll see just how much of a prima facie case the local talent's put together."

His eyes screwed up like a jeweler spotting a fakeroo. "I suppose you have a legal background," he sneered.

"I have. And certified to practice in Federal Courts. I'm no jaw-smith but I know how to derail something as simple as an arraignment. After that the fix doctor can take over." I turned to Allegra. "Appoint me attorney of record. Meadows here has practically pleaded Sonny guilty. He's got his long-term local relationships with the law to think of, but I haven't. I say Sonny stays right here. For his own good."

She stared at me uncertainly, then turned slowly to Attorney Meadows. "Paul," she said, "you see how it is ...."

He nodded stiffly. "Very well, Allegra, to spare you embarrassment I'll withdraw from the case. As of now." He picked up a briefcase from the table and walked away.

I took Allegra's hand. "Look," I said quietly, "I'm only a night-school lawyer but I'm not afraid to mix it with the locals and right now that's what Sonny needs. Looking at it another way, I can't possibly do anything to prejudice his chances. They decide murder cases on evidence, not manners."

She nodded slowly, her eyes widened, and she said, "I'm sure you'll do what's right, Steve." Then she turned from me and hurried out of the room.

White Ducks had stopped talking with the policeman. I walked over to the desk sergeant and said, "My name's Bentley. I'm acting as Mr. Tyner's attorney until you hear otherwise."

He scratched a notation on the police blotter.

"Mr. Tyner's not going to San Juan, Sergeant. We'll handle everything right here."

The Federal man came over to me, bristling. I said, "Your job's done, soldier, however poorly. There'll be no change of venue. We'll see the thing through right here. And afterward you'll be lucky if we don't hale you into court on charges of false arrest."

"Don't threaten me," he said angrily.

I laughed shortly. "That's a hell of a request from a cop who's just had an innocent man arrested. A prima facie case, is it? Let's see the color of your money."

His face darkened. "You'll wait for that, Counselor." The title had a sneer in it.

"Why not hold the pretrial hearing right now? Call your witnesses, ready your evidence, and I'll do the same."

He said, "I'm not the prosecuting attorney."

"You've been acting like one." I motioned him away from the desk, shook out a cigarette and lighted it. "Let's stop all the fur-bristling and get practical before it's too late."

"How do you mean, 'too late'?"

"I'm an old Treasury hand. That means I've palled around Washington with a lot of your gang. I've got a world of respect for your outfit but you're not infallible. You're not infallible because nobody is. Think back to the one detail that loused up the Judy Coplon case."

He groaned.

"Exactly," I said. "The guy forgot to get a warrant before he put the arm on Judy. Now, the people you work for are famous for having low boiling points. The guy who made that little slip-up with the warrant—ever hear of him again?"

"Nobody did."

"You're getting the point. Now let's hit some fundamentals."

An interested expression was growing in his eyes.

I said, "I want to see Reba's murderer caught and punished. So do you. On that much we agree. Where we disagree is who the murderer was. You must think you've got enough on Sonny to hang him or he wouldn't be in a cell right now. That's your right and it's your job as well. On the other hand I know Sonny. He's not entirely blameless in some of the things he's done but I'd bet a good chunk he never harmed Reba. If the court convicts Sonny you'll get another gold star in your personnel file. But if he's freed you'll have one hell of a lot of explaining to do—to hard-minded men who don't even listen to excuses. There'll be no gold star in the file then. There'll be a notation, though. Not much of a one, but enough to see that you're passed over and given dusty details for the next five years."

He rubbed the side of his nose thoughtfully. "What do you want?" he said finally.

"I want to know on what evidence Mr. Tyner has been accused of Reba's murder."

Taking my elbow he drew me farther away from the desk, into a corner of the room. "You bastard," he said with a half-smile, "you're giving me the shakes. I'm up for promotion in four months. If it goes through I can get married."

"You can still make it," I said, "but not by bringing Sonny Tyner to trial."

He lowered his voice. "Reba's ring," he said. "She wore one on the wedding finger, the one that was hacked off. The ring was found in Sonny's bureau drawer and brought here today."

I let a lot of air out of my lungs. I was sobering fast. That one was like the slap of an ice-cold towel.

"Who brought it in?"

"One of the maids at The Lodge. Norah Roberts."

"What else?"

"Her handbag, too."

"Prints?"

He shook his head. "Wiped clean. Some crusted blood, though. I expect the lab to show it was Reba's."

"Go on."

"He had time enough that night to do it. His story of stumbling home and falling asleep isn't substantiated. That answers the legal requirement for opportunity."

"Motive?"

He shrugged. "Jealousy, I guess. Jealous that she was sleeping with Dominic."

I nodded slowly. "For a circumstantial case it's pretty plausible. What's your name, by the way?"

"Hulik, Sam Hulik."

"Sam," I said, "there's something wrong with this one. From your point of view Sonny's guilty, but I don't believe it. For one thing he'd broken up with Reba months ago. It was all over."

"Yeah? He made a grab for her at Dominic's bar. You saw it—you were sitting beside him."

"Sonny'd been drinking, Sam. Reba sort of flounced past him and tried to give him a hard time. He wasn't having any of it. The drinks dissolved his inhibitions."

"Sure. But to what extent? I say he followed her after she left Dominic's, coaxed her down to the beach and stabbed her. With or without words being passed. The fact that he took a knife with him means premeditation. First-degree murder."

I put my rump on the top of a low chair and rested my weight. I looked up at him and said, "Big Sam, I don't buy any part of it."

He shrugged. "That's how it lays."

"I'm obliged for your telling me but actually you've just done yourself a favor. I'm going to juggle the elements and see what kind of a solution pops out."

"Sounds easy," he said in a needling way.

"We'll see. Right now I'll beg attorney's privilege and see my client."

"Good luck," he said and walked away.

The last quarter of an hour had cleared away the cottony miasma in my brain. The day's drinking was behind me. Shortly things should start to click.

A turnkey took me back to Sonny's cell and brought me a stool to sit on. I explained how I had happened to replace Mr. Meadows and Sonny said, "Thank God someone believes in me. I don't think even Allegra does."

I told him what evidence they had against him and how I had persuaded Hulik to tell me. Then I said, "Let's get one thing straight. I'm on your side all the way—unless I happen to discover something that convinces me you killed Reba. If that ever happens I'll be on the other side and I'll be wanting you to get the full extent of the law."

His hands gripped the bars and he pulled himself off the bunk. "Fair enough," he said in a hoarse voice. "I didn't kill her, Steve. I don't know how the ring and bag came to be in my dresser drawer. I can't be certain of every detail that night after I left you, but I know I went up to The Lodge and turned in. I never saw Reba again."

"This girl Norah Roberts. Ever have any trouble with her?"

He thought for a moment. "Not really. A couple of times guests were missing small things—tie clasps, earrings—stuff that could have been lost in the laundry. We had nothing against Norah. Sort of a brooding, silent type. Not very cheerful about anything."

"Think Norah could have planted those things in your drawer?"

"Anyone could have. It's not hard to get in and out of The Lodge without being seen. There's a back entrance, you know, and another around the side. Down here locked doors are almost unknown." His voice was measured, earnest. The voice of a man in deadly trouble.

"Not much there," I said and tried a smile. "In the meantime, keep hold of yourself. I'll have Allegra phone New York and get the best available criminal lawyer down here."

"Thanks, Steve," he said humbly. "I'll never forget this."

"Neither will I. For your sake I hope you'll be around to remember it for the next fifty years."

I got up, picked up the stool and the turnkey unlocked the hall door to let me out. He took the stool from me and sat down. "I hope you can help Mistah Tyner," he said in an undertone. "I don' believe he ever done harm to nobody."

"Thanks for the vote of confidence. I don't think he ever did either."

Simon Hargrave was pacing nervously beside the desk. When he saw me he bustled over and said. "Look. Bentley. I don't hold with what you're doing. Meadows is a capable lawyer. I wouldn't trust your legal training from here to the far wall. He wanted to get Sonny to San Juan for his own safety. You don't live around here, you wouldn't understand what's liable to happen."

"As usual," I said, "you've selling me short, Hargrave. High-priced, experienced criminal law talent is practically on the plane for Sonny. I could mention more but ethics forbid."

His face colored. He glowered at me and tried again. "I'm going to talk to Sonny."

Turning to the desk sergeant, I called, "See that no one except Mrs. Tyner gets to see Mr. Tyner."

The sergeant nodded.

Hargrave's fists clenched. "I get your game, Bentley. You want a cut of the big fee for defending Sonny."

I let my arms hang loosely at my sides. "Don't push me much further, Pop. Just another slim millimeter and you'll have me pulling your nose in public while the crowd roars." I stared at him. "The redhead, too."

His mouth went slack.

"You're all bluster, Hargrave, and blind to the fact that a man doesn't need a Cambridge accent to be a worthwhile citizen. I've known toffs before but you could take some schooling from Sonny in how to be a gentleman."

Then I stepped around him and walked outside.

Parked near the doorway was the low-slung Hargrave Mercedes. In it a girl in sun glasses. As she turned her head sunlight moved like fire through her red tresses. I walked up to her, leaned over and said, "You've got a date tonight, Irish."

"I know I have."

"This one's with me."

Her head tilted. "Sorry, Steve."

"Break it," I said. "Come up to The Lodge tonight. About nine."

She laid one hand on mine and spoke softly and seriously, "Steve, don't make things difficult for me. I thought you understood how things were."

"That doesn't mean I have to like them. Neither does it mean I'm trying to interfere. Sonny's in jail. Charged, as you know, with killing Reba Royce. I think he's innocent."

"What does that have to do with me?"

I patted her hand. "I'm giving you a chance to do something useful," I said. "Make a contribution to the human race. A chance like that doesn't come along every day."

"No," she said thoughtfully, "it doesn't. But what could I do, Steve?"

"Help save a man's life." Walking away, I didn't look back because about that time Hargrave would be coming out of Fort Christian, his breathing and blood pressure almost normal.

Somewhere I had left a drink. I started for the place but as I started to cross the square I saw two women coming out of the swinging doors: one old, one young. Sybil Dominic half-carrying her mother toward the Hillman convertible. Vane's joyous drinking had caught up with her and now her daughter was carting her off to the showers. A lot of that sort of thing and a daughter could start to question parental authority. I thought about offering a helping arm but Sybil seemed to have her mother under control. From the skillful way she managed I judged that it was almost a routine.

Changing course, I began walking up the hill to The Lodge.

CHAPTER THIRTEEN

The Tyner parrot was dipping his beak in an ash tray and gobbling cigarette butts. It eyed me challengingly. I murmured, "No objections, friend. Just no accounting for tastes."

Its honed beak flipped a mangled butt upward and caught it skillfully. The butt disappeared down its crop. To the last brown shred. Just watching the spectacle dried out my throat. I got up from the porch hammock, wandered over to the bar and mixed myself a peg of rum and fruit juice. The parrot had tackled another butt. I winged an ice cube at it, the poacher rasped loudly and fluttered up to its ceiling sanctuary.

Allegra Tyner came onto the porch, eyes reddened and weary even in the shadows. She said, "Steve, are you sure you want me here? I mean you and Kelly—"

"Stuff," I said. "She's an attractive young baggage but Hargrave leads me by a wide green margin. I know my place by now."

She smiled wanly. "I'm glad someone can do a little kidding. And thanks for phoning New York. What plane is Jamieson coming on?"

"Depends what he can catch out of Idlewild tonight. He'll be here in the morning or by mid-afternoon. Drink?"

"Might as well be loaded as the way I feel. Only nothing complicated, Steve."

I poured light rum into an old-fashioned glass, added a dash of bitters for vitamins and carried it over to her. She swirled the mixture for a moment, then drank deeply. After that she said,

"You were pretty rough on Meadows. What was all that about a jaw-smith and a fix doctor?"

"Yegg talk. Just to worry him."

"The circles you move in. I hate thinking about Sonny down in that cell. All alone."

"He's hardly alone. I saw plenty of spiders and roaches around."

"*Steve!*"

"Anyway, he won't be there long—and afterward he'll be the star of the Island cocktail circuit with stories of serving time in a tropical jail. A little imagination and he can blow up the story bigger than a dollar balloon."

"You sound awfully certain."

"And so I am. The experience won't hurt him, Allegra. It could even humble him a little and that wouldn't be bad, either."

A car had stopped on the road below. I heard the door open and close and in a few minutes light footsteps ascended the stairway. My wristwatch showed five after nine. For the Islands, Kelly was a punctual guest.

She came onto the porch, a lithe figure in a dark-green linen dress, half-heel shoes and a handbag. Walking to Allegra she said, "I'm Kelly Martin, Mrs. Tyner."

Allegra extended her hand. "I'm very glad you could come."

Kelly sat down beside her and looked across at me. "Hello, soldier. Still got chips on your shoulder?"

"Like a lumberjack."

She grimaced prettily, said, "Scotch for me," took a cigarette from her bag and lighted it. While I mixed a drink she and Allegra chatted inconsequentials. Then I carried over her drink and the maid passed around a tray of little sausages wrapped in crisp bacon and pine-apple splinters. Hawaiian motif.

I heard Allegra ask, "Will you be staying long in Saint Thomas?"

"I haven't very much choice. To put it bluntly, Mrs. Tyner, I'm flat broke."

I walked toward them from the bar. "But with prospects," I murmured.

"Oh, go to hell," Kelly snapped.

Allegra said, "Steve can be perfectly bestial."

Kelly smiled silkily. "As if I didn't know."

The maid finished passing the tray, put it down on the coffee table and left the porch.

Allegra said, "Sorry I'm such bad company tonight."

"I understand, Mrs. Tyner," Kelly said comfortingly. "Steve tells me all this will pass very quickly."

"I hope so," Allegra said distractedly, and finished her drink. Then she stood up. "I really ought to be down with Sonny, so if you children will forgive me, the place is yours."

"Of course," Kelly said. I moved over beside her and we watched Allegra cross the porch and start down the stairs. When her footsteps had faded Kelly looked up and said, "What on earth's it all about, darling? Why was my presence so essential here tonight?"

I sat down and lighted a cigarette. "You noticed the maid who passed the hors d'oeuvres?"

"Vaguely."

"Well, her name's Norah Roberts. Directly or indirectly she's responsible for Sonny's being in jail."

Her face whitened. "How?"

I told her. When I had finished, she sipped her drink, put it down and said, "What do you want me to do?"

"Norah doesn't live here at The Lodge. I want to know where she goes when she leaves here. If I were noticed following her I could manage only a seedy explanation. You won't be noticed at all, or questioned."

"Anything else?"

"You late-dating Hargrave tonight?"

"Perhaps."

I nuzzled the lobe of her left ear and she shivered slightly. "We-ell—perhaps not."

"Much better. Find out what you can about your target and report to me later."

"Where?"

"Silly girl."

"Animal." Her lips brushed my cheek as lightly as the wings of a moth. After we had nuzzled a while I said, "Norah's off at nine-thirty. From the post office you can spot anyone coming down the hill. Take her from there."

"What if Simon happens to see me?"

"Ignore him. Any other questions?"

In a hushed voice she said, "You're positive Sonny didn't kill Reba?"

I nodded.

"That's good enough for me, Steve. I didn't realize you were a lawyer, too."

"I passed the Bars once, that's about all. Anyway, a real legal eagle's arriving tomorrow: Tremayne Jamieson of Number One Wall Street."

"I've heard of him, I think."

"He's the best talent money can buy, Irish. Plus that he's a millionaire bachelor and still under forty-five."

"Interesting," she mused.

Patting her hand, I said, "Post time."

Nodding, she finished her drink and stood up.

I touched her handbag. "Got Little Nemo with you?"

"Yes."

"I'll take him."

"Steve—"

"Don't argue with the man."

Shrugging, she opened the bag and took out her pistol. All told it was nearly as big as my hand. A lady-size .32 Beretta, a garter gun. Not a roscoe for the heavy work, but a belly shot could make someone wince. Snapping the bag shut, she said worriedly, "What are you going to do?"

"I'm still thinking it over."

"Try not to get hurt, Steve."

"Take no odds on that." I dropped the pistol in my pocket, took her in my arms and kissed her cheek and the tip of her nose. "Good girl," I said. "Be off with you."

Turning, she left me and crossed the porch. I watched her go, feeling as though the circus had just left town. Her footsteps faded away and I went over to the bar and made another drink. I began thinking about her. Kelly and Simon. I tossed off the drink quickly. Nothing there for me. Now or ever. The best thing I could do would be to finish my work here and get back where I belonged.

Norah Roberts shuffled onto the porch and picked up the hors d'oeuvres tray. When she saw nobody but me she blinked and said, "You want more of these, Mr. Bentley?"

"No thanks, Norah. You can go now."

She nodded, turned and went back toward the kitchen. It would be her last chore at The Lodge. By now Sonny would have told Allegra about her.

The big house was as quiet as a vault at midnight. I thought of Victor Polo's naked corpse floating in the water. I thought about the horror that had been Reba's dead face and I visualized Ralph Dominic wading into the water for perhaps his last swim. Down in the shadows of the post-office arcade Kelly was waiting for Norah Roberts to come down from the hill and walk toward her home. Or would she go there directly? In a little while I would know the answer to that one.

Assuming that Sonny was innocent of Reba's death meant the ring and bag had been planted in his drawer. Norah's finding them and taking them to the police was a plausibly public-spirited act—if she hadn't planted the evidence herself. If she had, from where had the evidence come but from the murderer?

Somewhere at the back of the house a door shut softly, almost surreptitiously. I butted my cigarette, went over to the sofa and sat down. Picking up a magazine I leafed through it—stage business in case Norah peered in at me as she passed the porch.

Supposing Norah had done the planting and made the discovery, it was reasonable to assume the murderer would want a report from her now that Sonny was in jail. He would want details of everything that had been said and done at The Lodge today.

I was building a case on speculation, but with Sonny behind bars the murderer might get smug and take chances, unwise chances. I hoped he would.

At nine-forty I left the porch, went down the long stairway and climbed into the Volks. Releasing the brake, I let it coast down the hill until I could see the front of the post office. A couple was embracing in the shadows, nothing else. Kelly was gone.

Silently wishing her luck, I turned on the ignition and engaged the clutch. The motor exploded softly and I turned right on Main Street toward Frenchtown.

At the rim of the sea the moon was a newly minted silver dollar, distant and icily cold. From The Gate came the sound of Calypso revelry. The steel band sounded like bamboo tribal drums in a jungle clearing. What else you got out of it depended on your mood.

Coffee taverns, restaurants and apothecary shops were still open, but the rest of Charlotte Amalie had closed down. An occasional guest house on the hill showed a string of outdoor lanterns. Bamboushay—have yourself a big gutty time. The tourist slogan. I ought to come back once and bamboushay the hell out of the Virgin Islands. I ought to do a lot of things. What I was going to do had to do with the borrowed .32 Beretta in my pocket. I hated depriving Kelly of it but I would probably need it more than she.

Where I was heading had to do with the sudden transition of Sybil Dominic from a distraught wife into a female enjoying peace of mind. It had to do with where she went after she left Polo's Casino. You're sick, Sybil, I said half-aloud, but there's nothing basically wrong with you a divorce and a change of scene can't cure.

Dominic's hold over his wife defied analysis unless you reverted to the old theory of evil attracting good. Anyhow, that wasn't my problem. Domestic tensions were way out of my line. Particularly tonight.

Beyond the edge of town my lights picked up a solitary figure shuffling along the highway shoulder. They showed a man in a high-crowned hat, shapeless black pants and a shirt as red as red lipstick. Old Henry, no less, and minus his guitar. As I passed him I saw that his eyes were fixed on the dusty border. Fifty yards beyond I peered into the rear-view mirror. No Henry. Slowing, I made a U-turn and headed back. A car came toward me but its lights showed only bare road.

I idled along and spotted an access lane leading up the hill. Against the lighter dirt I could see movement. Henry was climbing the lane. Braking, I glanced at my watch and let the car ease over onto the shoulder. Leaving the parking lights on, I slid out of the Volks and crossed the highway. There was enough moonlight that I could pick my way without stubbing my toes.

A hundred yards above the highway the lane straightened and leveled off and I could spot Henry moving past the dim lights of a house. It was a wide, one-story rambler with wall-sized picture windows now curtained from the inside. Beside the path a mailbox bore letters that glowed dully in the moonlight. The name was *S. Hargrave*.

Ahead of me I could hear pebbles grating under Henry's feet as he walked around the side of the house. Moving close to the shrubbery, I saw a shaft of light split the darkness. It stabbed outward like a searchlight, I heard the low mutter of voices and then the light went out. The door closed.

Still hugging the shadows, I heard Henry's voice humming a disconnected song. In the night it sounded like an idiot crooning in a dark cell. The hair on the back of my neck began to prickle.

Henry passed me, still crooning, and shuffled down the path. When he had passed the mailbox I started after him, keeping on the grass border.

At the turn the house was blocked from sight. The old Negro was only a dozen feet ahead of me when I called, "Going to Frenchtown, Henry?"

I could hear his feet skid on the gravel. His voice quavered, "Who … who's that? I can't see."

Stepping onto the path I went up to him. He stood in the moonlight rigid with 'fear, something clutched between his two hands. His mouth opened and closed. His eyes recognized me and he sighed, "Oh. Thought you was maybe Mistah Hargrave."

"I'm just the fellow you're always meeting up with in the darkness."

"What you doin' here, mon?" he mumbled.

"Wondering what you're doing, Henry."

I was so close I could see his tongue lick his lips. Holding out one hand I said, "I'll take that."

"It's mine. All of it's mine." A panicky, unhappy voice.

I stared at him. Henry's eyes darted from side to side. He was thinking of bolting but he gave up the idea. Slowly, torturedly, his hands separated and surrendered a tattered old billfold. He hadn't quite finished what he had been doing with the billfold. And what he had been doing was stuffing a deck of ten-dollar bills inside it. I riffled through them and counted five. Fifty bucks. For Henry a fortune. "Come here often?" I asked.

His feet moved nervously. Pebbles rolled and the sound was like earth rattling against the top of a coffin. Dominic's coffin.

Henry husked, "I come once before."

I glanced down at the billfold, evened the edges of the bills and the glint of a celluloid card holder caught my eye. My free hand snapped my lighter and I saw a smudged Social Security card behind the scarred celluloid facing. It bore a long serial number and a typed name. I stared at the name until the lighter flame began to fade. Then I clicked it off. The Social Security card was in the name of Henry Royce.

Slowly I gave him back his billfold. "Reba's father," I said in a cracked voice.

His feet shuffled again. "Yessah." His fingers clutched the billfold and jammed it into his hip pocket. His eyes were half-moons, flecked with fear.

"What do you do for Simon Hargrave that's worth mint moss, Henry?"

His mouth opened and shut. His face turned away.

I laughed shortly. "I could slap you around until you told me but I think I know."

His head screwed around and his face twitched. "You know?"

"Sure. Reba had lovers. Among them Sonny Tyner and Ralph Dominic and at least one other—Simon Hargrave."

"That's right," he managed in an awed voice. "Only Mistah Hargrave don' want no one to know 'bout it."

"I can imagine. Now take a little advice. Don't think what you know about Hargrave means the world by the tail. The mistake blackmailers make is getting too greedy. When they do the victim starts to plan how to get rid of his problem. Be reasonable with him, Henry, and this could go on for quite a long time."

"Yessah."

"Also," I said, "don't take any chances. Stick to lighted streets and watch what they drop in your drinks. Hargrave home?"

"Nossah."

"That'll be all, Henry."

Blinking, he turned and started down the hill again. I stood there until the sound of his footsteps blurred and faded into the tropical night.

Taking a deep breath, I shook myself and stared out over the sea. The moon was higher now, a Cyclops' eye, serrated and blind. It was a castaway's moon and I was the only living man on a jungle island. Shivering in the cool dampness, I began picking my way down the hill. At the bottom I found the Volks and crawled behind the wheel. Then I started the engine, turned around and drove on toward Frenchtown.

CHAPTER FOURTEEN

The revelation that Simon had enjoyed a left-handed honeymoon with Reba would interest Sam Hulik and the police. It was significant enough to start them investigating in a new direction—one that could end with Hargrave in Sonny's cell and Sonny back on his own veranda tippling banana squash. I thought of the scribbled note I had found in Reba's wastebasket. Sonny had denied writing it, so it might well be Hargrave's. I wondered where he was tonight.

At the Crown Mountain road I turned up, following the serpentine ruts, the Volks bucking the steep incline and almost standing on its rear wheels. Once I glimpsed Magens Bay in the moonlight. Its rim of sand lay starkly white against an oily black sea. A dead world viewed through a high-powered telescope. Foliage cut off the image and the Volks plowed onward.

I drove as far as I thought prudent and braked the Volks half off the road. Taking the trouble flashlight, I got out and began walking toward the access road that led to the hug house that Sonny had bought for Reba.

Stillness surrounded me, not even the flutter of a bird against a leaf. My footsteps sounded enormously loud and I slowed and picked my way more carefully. Where the access drive began I flashed on the light, knelt and swept the loose dirt. Tire tracks stood out in perfect impacted patterns. A lot of tire tracks and probably by two different cars. I wondered if one of the cars would still be parked beside the bungalow.

Flicking off the light, I stuck it in my pocket, felt for Kelly's Beretta and slid a shell into the chamber. Pistol in hand I went the rest of the way. Very slowly and quietly.

Only a little moonlight filtered through the vaulting branches. Overhead trailing lianas formed grotesque silhouettes: ships' cables, monkeys' tails, jungle snakes, hangman's ropes. The air was close and fetid as an old slaughter house.

In the darkness I could barely make it out. The house was entirely dark and no car was parked in the little clearing. Somewhere a faucet was dripping. The drops fell in a precise monotonous rhythm, like the measured ooze of blood. I shivered again. Then I went to the garage and began working my way around the back of the house. The aluminum window louvers were closed. Once something caught my foot and I almost yelled but when I freed myself I felt a coil of plastic garden hose. My heart was pounding and it took more than a couple of deep breaths to get it back to normal.

Stepping around the kitchen door, I paused beside each window, listening, until I had completed the circuit of the house. The front door was locked, of course, so I walked back to the kitchen door and began to pry at the door bolt with the Volks key. I might as well have saved myself the effort because the bolt was in its recess and the door opened easily. The unlocked door was something different. Different but not entirely unexpected.

Stepping quickly into the dark kitchen, I shouted, *"Dominic!"*

My throat was tight. I wet my lips and called, "Come out, Dominic. Sybil's told the cops you're here. You'll get a better break if you turn yourself in. I'm here to take you back."

It was a long speech. Loud and a little blustery. I wondered if it kidded anyone into thinking I wasn't scared.

It was much too long a speech for the answer it got. Not even the creak of a board or the sound of the front door answered me. I wondered if I had guessed wrong. My hunch had been based on the change in Sybil. I had figured that she had located Dominic, and from the direction she had driven and the length of time she had been out of sight I had placed him here in Reba's Roost. Only Dominic didn't have to have come here. There were a dozen other cottages on Crown Mountain where he could have hidden out, but because he had been Reba's lover I assumed he knew this place was vacant.

Gripping the .32, I moved slowly through the littered kitchen toward the living-room door. Before I passed through I stood beside the door frame and called Dominic's name again. Still no answer. Near my feet something scuttled away with a rasping sound and when I had crawled down from the ceiling I realized it was only a mouse. Sucking my heart back out of my throat, I went through the door frame into Reba's living room.

The room was totally dark. I palmed the wall for a light switch but found none. With my left hand I pulled the flashlight from my pocket and sprayed the beam around.

The furniture was where it had been before, impersonal and tawdry. In front of the gaudy sofa the rattan coffee table held a dirty plate, a knife and fork and an open beer can. In the last two days someone had eaten here. That explained the open kitchen door. I thought about picking up the beer can to see if it had been drained but decided against smudging the finger-prints. Turning, I played the light around the room, looking for more traces of recent living and then my breath stuck in my throat.

The ceiling of the room arched over heavy horizontal cypress rafters spaced about six feet apart and at a height of ten or twelve feet. Around one of them had been tied a length of plastic gar-den hose that hung straight down. It was stretched rigidly stiff because of the heavy burden noosed to the lower end.

A man hung there, like a dead bird throttled in a loop of string. Because his back was to me, all I could see was a soiled T-shirt, drab chino trousers and scuffed shoes. Around his neck the plastic hose had bitten so deep that the flesh swelled up and around, almost concealing it. Edging forward, I kept the light on the corpse until I could see the face.

It was a face I had seen before. Only not in the rictus of death. Not with bulging eyes and a tongue half bitten through. In life it had been the face of Ralph Dominic.

Slowly, with effort, I began to breathe again. All my senses were alert now, keyed to the least sound, the slightest motion. I levered the beam away from Dominic's staring eyes and slanted it to the floor, looking for the chair or a stool from which he could have stepped to his death. Then I walked until I was close enough to touch his hand. The fingers were slightly flexed but when I tried to bend them they resisted. The joints were frozen with rigor. The body swayed slowly and began to turn. I stepped away and felt my stomach roll over.

Across the top of Dominic's forehead stretched a blue-black mark raised and swollen like a leech. Either he had fallen and bruised himself or he had been sapped. I was getting a reasonably clear idea of how he had come by his bruise.

My fingers had clenched the pistol painfully tight. Loosening them, I snapped off the flashlight and went back through the kitchen. Pushing the door outward, I stepped onto the grass and let it swing shut silently. So much for Reba's Roost and the hanged man inside. My mind was recovering from the shock. I was beginning to put together combinations and events, working back from a single concept of cause and effect. But I was thinking at the wrong time, thinking when I should have been watching and listening.

As I rounded the corner of the house, something whistled through the air and glanced off the left side of my head onto my collarbone. Sparks of pain rocketed through the night and I realized dimly that the flashlight had dropped from numbed fingers. I was on my knees, dazed and fighting to get upright, trying to get my back against the house for protection, when I saw the bulk of a man in front of me. His face was only a blur but I could see his arm outlined above his head. There was something in his hand. A bludgeon smashing at my head. But my right arm was still mine, the fingers responded and from the hip I shot him.

Sound bellowed out, red flame seared the air between us and I heard an agonized shout. In a sick flash I knew the little pistol had been too small for the job. The wall collapsed on my head and I pitched forward.

Smoke filled my lungs. Choking, I sucked more smoke. Then I vomited. Rolling over, I grasped emptily for the pistol but it was gone. I could hear the harsh crackle of flames. The ground beneath me was stone hard and smooth. My hand felt it. Not ground, not grass and cool earth but warm flooring. The smoke was strangling me. I managed to get to my knees. My eyes were open now; sick, incredulous eyes that stared at flames licking toward me from the kitchen. I was in the living room, not far from Dominic's still body. Panic gripped me and I staggered upright and stumbled toward the front door. Fumbling with the bolt, I clawed it open and pushed out. Coughing and retching, I fell forward onto the grass. My fingers dug into it prayerfully as my lungs pumped fresh air into my blood. A sudden flicker of flames stabbed through the open door, fed by the new draft. Digging my fingers into the sod, I bellied myself toward the shadows, praying my attacker wasn't waiting there to finish me. My gun was gone, so was the flashlight. I was alone and sick and defenseless.

The slant of the land helped me and finally I reached a tree and pulled myself erect. My skull bones felt looser than a bag of dice. Dazedly I propped myself against the tree and concentrated on breathing. Dominic's body was back there, the fire would obliterate the evidence and ... but getting poisoned air out of my lungs was the first thing I had to do. Nausea rose but I forced it back. A miasma of smoke and stinking vomit swirled through my brain. Dominic's murderer had come back and the parked

Volks had given my presence away. So instead of just burning the bungalow to do away with Dominic's body he had sapped me and dragged me inside. Tomorrow there were to have been two charred corpses and a gun. It was to have been a setting the police could interpret as they pleased. And all of it leading away from the real murderer.

But the bad note for him was the gunshot wound. His cry told me I had winged him. Finding him would be easier now. A lot easier.

Desperate last-ditch strength stiffened my legs. Pushing away from the tree, I tottered down the drive toward the road. From the house flames crackled and roared upward. A pyre for Ralph Dominic.

Under my uncertain feet loose stones rattled and rolled. I was making a lot of noise but I was too far gone to care. Either he would kill me before I reached the Volks or I would gain it and find strength in the whisky bottle. A nerve in my face began to twitch. I giggled crazily and blinked. Not much farther. Ten yards more and you've got it made.

Behind me a dull glow rose above the burning house. Soon sparks would dart upward and the roof would cinder and cave in. By then the fire department would be on the way. By then I would be a long way from Crown Mountain.

The Volks was wet with dew. I grabbed the door, pulled it open and collapsed behind the wheel. Groggily I reached into the glove compartment and pulled out the pint. Slowly, interminably, I unscrewed the metal cap. Then, closing my eyes, I rested back against the seat cushion, tilted my head and let the whisky trickle into my mouth.

Swallowing without retching took a mountain of effort, but I managed a good two ounces before my gorge finally rose. Hands on the wheel, I pulled myself forward, set my teeth and started the engine.

In the jungle around me birds were chattering and bustling as though dawn had come. I grimaced, wheeled the Volks around and steered it slowly down the road. Each jar seemed to lift the top of my skull and slam it against the metal roof, but the liquor was steadying me now, dulling my brain.

I thought of driving down to the Normandie Bar for an ice pack and a look around but I wasn't ready to have it known that I survived. Henry Royce was a dull-witted blackmailer but not a killer. Not unless I figured him wrong. He hadn't slugged me at Reba's house because on foot he couldn't have gotten there in time. All that Henry Royce had was a sniggering secret and an outstretched hand. I liked learning of Simon Hargrave's affair with Reba. I liked it a lot. Since sundown it was the only thing that hadn't hurt and so far as I was concerned old Henry could keep tapping Hargrave until death ended the arrangement.

Another hairpin turn, back wheels skidding, lights jerking across dark walls of foliage. Then the road straightened and dipped down onto the highway. What information I had for Sam Hulik and the police could wait a while. Until I had it organized. Until the thought processes got re-established in my battered brain. By now Sonny was asleep. Let him sleep. Some things were done by night. Truth was a daytime thing. Truth could wait for morning.

The Volks seemed to be creeping over a dusty black ribbon that led toward lights speckling the harbor hillside. Kelly should be in her room by now. I wanted to know what she had found out. I needed it to piece together what I already knew and guessed. And I wanted soft hands doing things for me, caring for a tattered cavalier. At the first road I turned toward the waterfront and headed for Dominic's.

Parking the Volks, I got out and tottered toward the back stairs. The dance combo was groaning something old and familiar. Something I couldn't place. Along with everything else it seemed unimportant. Up the stairway and into the familiar hallway. I opened her door and saw the glow of a cigarette in the darkness.

"Hello, Irish," I croaked.

"Hello, soldier," a calm voice said. "You took your time getting here. I've been back for hours."

I closed the door behind me and shot the bolt. "You came close to being a widow tonight. And I lost Little Nemo."

The bed lamp flicked on, making a low discreet glow. She was sitting upright, pillows propped behind her, wearing only a filmy bed jacket. "What happened?" she whispered.

"Trouble found me," I said heavily. "More than I could handle. Dominic's dead. The killer slugged me and locked me in a burning house. What's left of me feels like a dime's worth of yesterday's dog meat."

That brought her out of the bed. "God," she husked, "you look as though a truck ran over you."

I slumped onto the bed and blinked at her. My eyes weren't used to light yet, only to shooting stars. Her hand touched my head and drew back slowly. "You need a doctor," she said in the command voice females use when they begin to rise to an occasion.

"I haven't eaten my last sap yet. Wrap ice in a towel and lay it on my fevered brow. Then croon me a cradle song."

"*Steve*, be serious this once."

I waved my hand at the tray of drinks. Among other things it offered a bucket of ice cubes. Picking it up, she disappeared into the bathroom. As I lay back against her pillow I could hear the clink of cubes. She was qualifying rapidly as a wife and helpmate. Any more revealed talents and I would feel obliged to make an honest woman of her. Closing my eyes, I felt her place something cool and damp across my forehead. Then her lips brushed mine and she drew back. "You're stinking drunk."

"Possibly. Can you make Rhode Island Johnnycake?"

She laughed uncertainly. "Make it? I've never even heard of it."

"A shame. It's something from outer space. Drenched in maple syrup, of course."

"Oh, of course," she said dryly and I felt her untying my shoelaces.

"You like Chincoteague oysters?"

"Love them." My shoes came off.

"Well," I said, "that's a start. We could live on Chin-coteagues while I'm teaching you to make Johnnycake."

Her lips touched my aching forehead. "That's the most off-beat proposal I've ever heard It *is* a proposal, isn't it?"

"Nothing less."

The light clicked off and the bed gave as she lay down on the other side. "Steve," she said quietly, "let's not talk about it until morning. Don't you want to know what Norah Roberts did?"

"Sure."

Her hand found mine and our fingers laced. "Well, she walked about five blocks from the post office and went into a little taxi booth. I was too far away to see what she was doing—if she was doing anything at all. Then she came out and kept going to the house where she lives."

"She didn't ride in a taxi?"

"No. I guess it was just a waste of time."

"How little you know, Irish," I murmured and nuzzled her cheek. "Did you see Hargrave anywhere?"

"No. Do you think I'd—"

"Simmer down," I said, "put out the cat and let's knit the raveled sleeve. Tomorrow could be a busy, fretful day."

CHAPTER FIFTEEN

Lacy white clouds rode the morning sky. Birds rocketed through the trees and offshore a crowd of gulls were cutting up a school of racing fry. Breakfast was a plate of molten chili beans, a milkshake and a fistful of aspirins. My head felt like an anvil but I could focus, walk and take nourishment again. I was sound as a plugged nickel and ready for whatever the day might bring.

Kelly had been sleeping when I left, sleeping in the totally relaxed manner of kittens and small furry animals. Waking her would have been as heartless as it was unnecessary. And so I had simply shaved and gone out.

Because I had places to go, things to do. And I didn't want a lot of people watching me. So far as the killer who had coshed me knew I was lying in the ruins of Reba's bungalow, crisper than a strip of Kansas bacon. He could go on thinking that. For a while.

Checking the gas gauge, I got into the Volks and started the engine. I had been driving it for three days and the tank was still three-quarters full. The Volks used less than an atomizer and by now it seemed like an old friend. It had taken me in and out of more trouble than I wanted to remember and there was still more ahead.

I pulled away from the beanery and turned onto the airport road. Overhead the first flight from San Juan was banking into the landing pattern and I wondered if Lawyer Jamieson was aboard. Allegra would know. She would meet him or send Big John the way she had sent Big John to meet me. I thought about old Henry and his guitar and his alky breath and wondered what he had done with last night's fifty dollars. At two bits a drink the half century should see him through the week. Unless he invested it all in tarantula juice. As a payoff it wasn't much, but then it wasn't much of a secret either.

In daylight the private road was easier to find than last night when old Henry had trudged up to the big house at the top of the hill. A lot of expensive gardening had gone into the oleander borders and the lawn was as evenly trimmed as green velvet. House and grounds together couldn't have cost a guinea under ninety thousand dollars. Sunken sprinkler holes lifted little diamond umbrellas. A robber jay stabbed its beak into the spray and fenced with the droplets. Braking the Volks, I shut off the ignition and crawled out.

A drive led around the side of the house to a garage that held Hargrave's Mercedes. Parked by the garage and half out of sight was a teal-blue Hillman convertible. I didn't have to peer at the plates to know whose it was. Considering his age Hargrave was turning out to be quite a stud. Sybil for breakfast and Kelly for lunch. With Reba unavailable I wondered who the lucky evening lass might be.

The door knocker was wrought iron twisted into a design that might have meant something if you had time to ponder the meaning. I didn't. All I did was lift it and rap four times. Then I leaned against the side of the door and waited. It was the moment to light a cigarette, yawn and look blasé but last night's smoke would last me the rest of the year. The door was veined cypress, varnished and polished smooth. I rapped it again and did some more waiting. Somewhere inside the house I heard a woman laugh. The sound set my teeth on edge. Turning, I looked out over the highway and the little beach and beyond where emerald-green water undulated gently in the sunshine. Rising above it, Water Island looked near enough to touch. I turned around and stared at the knocker. I was getting ready to tear it off when the door opened.

His hair was tousled and his eyes were veined with red. Even a yard away his breath reeked whisky. He wore a blue oxford beach robe and a tangle of gray hairs poked through the open V at his throat. He looked like a man who had been sleeping off a wowser. His puffy lids narrowed and he rasped, "Get the hell out of here."

"Easy on the cuss words. A fellow your age ought to set an example for the younger generation—including the ladies." I stuck my foot in the door opening.

He jumped back. "What the hell is this?"

I grinned. "Hair combed and twenty years younger you could pass for Daddy Longlegs himself. But right now you look less toothsome than last week's barbecue. The fact that Mrs. Dominic flopped here last night doesn't shatter my young dreams. I didn't know she'd be here. What I happen to know is that you're paying off an old jake-hound to the extent of fifty skins a dip to guard a secret everyone'll know by noon today."

"You son of a bitch," he snarled.

"Fine," I said. "I'm a son of a bitch and you're a superannuated whoremaster. If you want to start throwing punches let's get it over with. Compared to the saps I've chewed lately anything you could muster would be limper than steamed spaghetti."

His mouth opened and closed. His eyes narrowed and then he blinked. His shoulders seemed to sag. Sullenly he said, "You can't prove a damned thing."

Reaching into my coat pocket, I got out my wallet and pulled out the scrap of notepaper I had been carrying. "I'm no graphologist, but comparing your signature on the Coco Isle papers with what's written here makes you the writer."

He managed a sneer. "What's that supposed to be?"

"A note you left for Reba at the Crown Mountain love nest."

He grabbed at it but I pulled it away. "Gently, Massah Hargrave. It's evidence."

His face was growing gaunt. "Evidence of what?"

"That you were one of Reba's lovers. They stuck Sonny in jail for not much more than that—oh, a frame was thrown in, but that was incidental to the theme. And you were such a good friend of Sonny's that you buttoned up and scuttled away. A real buddy."

"How much?" he grated.

"The logical question," I said, "if I were Henry Royce. But we're talking police business now. Try buying it from them."

His face had mottled. The cords in his neck stood out like tent ropes. He was working up a flowering case of apoplexy. I said, "There's nothing left at the lust lodge, Hargrave. Nothing but ashes and charred timber. And, of course, a corpse."

His eyes goggled. "Who …" he whispered. "Whose body?"

There was movement in the room behind him. The light padding of slippered feet. I could guess whose they were. "The lady's a widow," I said. "You tell her. It'll come better from a friend of the family."

His eyes were glazed. Slowly he turned away and I got my foot out of the way so that the door could shut. As I walked down the path I heard a piercing shriek come from the house. Then the sound of a woman babbling. So much for adultery. My mouth tasted like a barrel of rancid cheese.

I got into the Volks and put Hargrave's note back inside my wallet. It was time Sybil knew about it anyway. The police and her mother would have been looking for her since last night. Providing the flames had left anything identifiable as Ralph Dominic.

The masked jaybird had flown away. The little sprinkling jets made bright rainbows in the sunlight. Spaced along the oleander border were flamboyant trees, their blooms like bleeding hearts. I looked back up at the big expensive house and thought that it was a place to sleep in and drink in and then some night do the Dutchman with sleeping pills or a pistol to end the loneliness. But I could have been wrong.

At the foot of Hargrave's private road I turned onto the highway and headed for Frenchtown again. A taxi was bearing down on me. As it whizzed past I saw it carried a load of passengers from the airport. Tremayne Jamieson, the Boy Wonder, could be among them, for all I knew. I didn't really care. A little more work and the jail doors would swing open for Sonny Tyner. With or without Tremayne Jamieson, Esquire.

I wondered what the killer was doing now. He could be guzzling at the Normandie Bar or driving aimlessly or prowling through ashes on Crown Mountain. He could be doing anything at all. As I turned in past the old headstones I thought about Sam Hulik. He would be a good man to have along at the finish, a man to wrap up the package and fly it back to San Juan. But to construct any kind of a package there had to be proof, technical proof, or witnesses, and it was too late for that. Far too late. It had to be done another way, a way no Federal officer would touch. It had to be done my way.

Cha-Cha shed windows were propped open and skinny kids loitered behind screen doors. Smoke curled upward from a dozen washtub fires. An old Cha-Cha in overalls trudged along the rutted road toward the Normandie Bar. His scrawny neck was burned the color of fish guts. So long as the sea gave forth fish and his old woman could take in washing he had no problems. Not with shinny at ten cents a shot.

The clearing in front of the Normandie Bar was a baked plain, a setting for Custer's Last Stand. Easy, Bentley, grab a little oxygen and drift back to earth. There's work to be done. I gripped the wheel hard and angled onto the sandy path that led back through the overgrowth to Victor Polo's Casino.

By daylight I liked it better. I liked it better without Sybil Dominic wailing for a husband now dead; without Pierre Duroc watching through the underbrush. By daylight it was only another old, decaying house. Ghosts came only by night.

In case anyone was interested I left the Volks in plain sight in front of the Casino and pocketed the key. Then I opened the bonnet and took out a tire iron. Looking around, I saw only tall trees and a raft of lily pads drifting on the water. From branches and trailing vines the Spanish moss hung like the beards of dead men. I put my foot on the bottom step and began to climb, each step creaking a Celtic dirge until I was on the porch and picking my way around holes in the planking.

When I reached the door I put my hand on the board cross and pulled but it was nailed tight. With the tire iron I pried it down and it dropped on the porch with a loud clatter. Then I kicked the front door open.

Inside the air was cool and still. There was dust and little drifts of sand on the flooring and the furniture was covered with tatters of dry rot. The stairway to the second floor looked too feeble to climb so I passed it by and went through the foyer into what had been the game room. The tables were still there, the dice tables' green baize faded and peeling as though giant hands had scraped it away from the sunken top. The roulette layouts were shrunken and curling but where the creepers had spun only round holes were left. Under a table a broken chip rake lay on the dusty floor. Standing in the center of the big room, I had the sensation of being in a sunken ship. I shook myself and moved on.

The office door hung open. I tried to push it but it had warped fast against the flooring. In a far corner stood an open rusted safe. I went to it and peered past the heavy stepped door into the big box, and poked the tire iron inside. Dry paint flaked off in big leaves. The safe was emptier than a burlesque house on Easter Sunday.

As I straightened I could visualize the hour five years before when Victor Polo and Ralph Dominic had opened their safe and split their kitty. But they were dead now and no one could recreate the scene. Half-aloud I said, "You were a chump, Polo. You trusted a crook." Then I turned and went back through the door. The tire iron in my hand hung heavier than a saber.

The kitchen sported a big rusty range and an estate-size wooden ice-box now split and molded. The tinned table tops were corroded and the sinks grew more moss than a Japanese garden. Triple nightmares for Fanny Farmer.

Only one more room to go. Five years ago it would have been the storeroom. As I walked toward it I saw a Yale lock on the door. In front of the door the flooring was as clean of dust as though it had just been swept.

It was a sign I had been looking for. Gripping the tire iron I walked to the storeroom door and lifted the iron to pry the door open but it showed a quarter of an inch. Peering through the crack I could see light filtering through a high barred window. There seemed to be crates and boxes inside the room. My hand opened the door the rest of the way. It swung silently, on oiled hinges, I stepped across the threshold, blinked and froze.

The light that strained through the barred window was patterned by an overhang of creepers and vines. It was a gray shadowy light that showed a tall pile of boxes nearly surrounding an iron spring bed. It drifted onto a man sitting at the edge of the bed in chino pants and a T-shirt. The heel of his right hand rested on his right thigh and his fingers held a gun. I had seen the gun before, held by the same man. It was an Army .45 and the man was Pierre Duroc.

Thickly he said, "I wondered who the hell was mousing around. I mighta known it was you. Come on in. Easy, Bentley. Nothing sudden." He got up slowly and his tongue licked his lips.

"Barley belly himself. How's the contraband game these days?"

"Not bad," he said carefully. "Not bad except when I get snoopers about. Too bad for you, Bentley." The gun jerked up.

"Oh, put it away," I drawled. "I guess you heard me working the window the other night, tiptoed outside and slugged me."

He nodded. "I didn't know it was you till I shined the light."

"My tough luck. Well, I've been slugged harder since then."

He grunted. "That happens to snoopers."

"Sleep here last night?"

"Yeah. You just woke me. I sleep light."

I sucked in a deep breath. "You're the boss now," I said. "In case you hadn't heard."

His forehead wrinkled. "How's that?"

"Dominic," I said patiently. "Your partner. He's dead."

He laughed uncertainly. "Yeah? Everyone knows he took a long swim. You call that news?"

I shook my head. "I don't mean hiding out. I mean dead." I spelled the word for him, writing with one index finger in the air.

His eyes narrowed. "You got me half-believing it."

"The Crown Mountain shack is a pile of ashes today. Among the remains is a man's corpse. Dominic's. Turn on the radio or read it in the papers."

"How? Who done it?"

"I thought you'd know."

He took two steps toward me. "Don't get bright with me. I asked you a question. Who done it?"

"Who killed Victor Polo?" I asked. "Who killed Reba Royce?"

"Don't give me questions. I want answers." He took another step toward me. The Colt was only a yard away, pointing at my left side.

I said, "The Law would like a few words with you, Pierre. There's a nice stock of contraband here. With Dominic dead you're the only visible owner. That points to a motive."

His mouth twisted.

"Behind you!" I yelled.

He whirled around in quick reflex and as his gun arm swept back I chopped the tire iron onto his wrist. He shrieked and the Colt clattered onto the floor. Moaning and cursing, he went onto his knees but I kicked the gun away, lunged for it and grabbed it up.

Pierre had jammed his wrist against his mouth. There was sweat on his forehead, little droplets against skin that had suddenly turned gray. On his knees he made his way back to the bed and leaned against it, clamping his wrist with his left hand and rocking from side to side.

I bore down on him. "The picture changes," I snarled. "People are giving me guns so I'm all bowlegged carrying them. You're no gunslinger, Pierre. The act may get a big hand from the apple-knockers but it's a bust with me. On the bed and start talking."

Heavily he levered himself onto the bed and drew up his knees. Pain had shot streaks of white through his face. His right hand dropped like wet felt.

The dim light showed labels on the crates and boxes: Napoleon brandy, Spode China, Swedish crystal, Danish silver, French perfume, Wedgwood ... I looked down at Pierre Duroc.

"You broke my arm," he moaned.

"That's what a snooper can do," I jeered. "And you suckered for the oldest gaff alive. That's why you were the handyman and Dominic was the bankroll. There had to be a reason why Dominic didn't liquidate this place and sell it for lumber. An operator like Dominic wouldn't have let any kind of an asset stay idle. That meant it was being used for something. And Sybil coming here meant she had reason to think he might be around. I got slugged for taking a look and twice I found you here—once with a gun in your belt. Too much for coincidence, Pierre. Too much for just idle interest in an old deserted house. Now, we'll talk about Dominic."

His eyes were shot with hate. He elbowed himself up and spat at me.

I said, "If I've broken one arm I can break the other. We were talking about Dominic. The dead man."

His tongue licked his lips. His face twisted in pain and he grated, "All right. I took him to Reba's place."

CHAPTER SIXTEEN

"That's a start," I told him. "Keep it coming."

Breath whistled through his set teeth. It was the sound of a man in severe pain. Glancing down at his wrist, he gagged and peered up at me. "He had to disappear. We thought about how Polo was found and decided on the water trick. He left some clothes on the beach and walked down the sand. He kept on walking in the water and came back to the beach farther down. It was low tide. The water covered his tracks. Then I drove him in a truck up to Reba's. I left him there."

"Go on."

"I ain't seen him since."

"Who killed him?"

"How the hell do I know?"

"You can do better than that. Who killed Victor Polo, Pierre? You? Dominic?"

"Me, no. Dominic didn't say."

"What about Reba?"

He managed a tortured shrug.

I sat down on a crate and stared at him. "Three days ago you told me Polo had a bad name with women, then you got coy. I want the rest of the story and I want it now."

Heavily he said, "Polo got girls—told them he ran night clubs in South America. He sneaked them out of here and they never came back. You figure it out."

"I have. Did he know Reba Royce?"

"Maybe. Maybe no."

I said, "I like it Polo came back here to get his part of the split from Dominic and you or Dominic or both of you knocked him off. I like it Reba saw it happen—or found out about it and threatened to make trouble. Her father's a blackmailer, maybe it runs in the blood. Only Dominic was a tough guy who didn't threaten so good. I like it he killed her or had her killed and you knew about it. What I like best of all is tying you into the big finale with the bonfire last night. The big solution. And leaving you with a warehouse full of marketable goods."

His cheeks were cavernous. He almost screamed, "I didn't do it! None of it!"

"Then talk."

"Jesus, I don't know nothin'." The Cha-Cha twang had died out of his voice, leaving him just another busted monkey.

I stood up. "You son of a bitch," I snarled, "if I thought you tried to burn me last night I'd drill you in the belly and watch you puke out your life in your own bed."

Horror filled his eyes. "God, I swear I didn't do nothin'. I only helped Dominic move the goods. Nothin' more. You got to believe me. All I know is Dominic told me Reba knew somethin' about how Polo died. If he told me that much he didn't do it. It was somebody else."

"Who?"

"A boy friend, maybe. Jesus, Bentley, I don't know."

"She had more boy friends than an alley cat. Which one?"

He shook his head dumbly. Then he lay back on the bed and closed his eyes. His right hand was as bloodless as a slice of bread. Suddenly his arm went limp and his knees sprawled. Pierre Duroc had fainted.

I stared at him, grunted and turned around. Then I stuck the Colt in my pocket and walked out of the storeroom. Against my thigh the pistol was heavier than a cannon. The air was suffocatingly hot. It clogged my lungs and for a moment I got lightheaded.

Leaning against a roulette table until it passed, I stumbled on through the ruin of Victor Polo's hush joint and pushed out into the outside air.

My Volks was still there. Nothing had changed. From the glove compartment I pulled the pint bottle and drained an ounce where it would do the most good. My head was throbbing again and the action with Pierre had taken a lot out of me. I was weaker than I had imagined.

A boy friend of Reba's had killed her, Pierre guessed. I thought I knew which one.

Down the sandy lane, following the ruts of my own tires back toward the Normandie Bar. Inside I could see the same old clutch of bar buzzards. Outside Henry Royce lay in the shade of a tree. I got out of the Volks and went over to him. Squatting down, I shook his shoulder until his eyes opened. When he recognized me his face stiffened and he sat up. "Henry," I said, "let's talk business. Fifty bucks is a lot of money. Now, how'd you like five hundred?"

He stared at me blearily. "For what, mon?"

"Who killed Reba?"

His head moved slowly. "Do' know."

"Five hundred dollars, Henry. Fifty ten-dollar bills. Plus police protection. Tell me what you know."

His mouth moved. One scaly hand lifted and plucked vaguely at his cheek.

I said, "All right, we'll go at it another way. Did Victor Polo ever make a pass at Reba?"

He nodded slowly.

"Five years ago, or this time around?"

"Las' week. When Polo come back."

"You're starting to earn it. What did Reba do about it?"

"She? She wen' with him one night."

"The night Polo died?"

He nodded uncertainly.

"Look," I said patiently. "I know she didn't kill Polo. Reba didn't kill anybody. But she might have set it up for someone else to kill him. Now, did someone make her do that?"

He stared at me.

I pulled out my wallet, searched it and found ninety dollars. I laid them across his thigh. The convincer. He stared at the green bills and his eyes got big. He licked his lips. One hand clawed them up and jammed them into his pocket. His eyes grew crafty.

I said, "You'll get the rest, Henry. Now talk."

He wiped his mouth on his forearm. It would be a dry mouth, dry from gin and shinny rum. Slowly at first he began to talk. Memory sobered him and the words came easier. As I listened my legs cramped and I sat down beside him. I listened for what seemed like a long time. When he stopped talking, I got up and went into the Normandie Bar. Elbowing a space for myself, I tossed off a shot of rum with a sour lemon chaser and staggered out into the sunlight again. As I crawled into the Volks I saw that Henry was prone again, straw hat over his face. I wondered what had happened to his guitar. Hell, he was fixed now. Henry Royce was a capitalist.

Driving back into Charlotte Amalie, I began fitting the pieces together: what I had found out myself, what Pierre had told me and what I had learned from Henry Royce. Together it completed the puzzle. Now it was time for some Law. Time for Sam Hulik and the locals to sweep up. And time for me to take a rest.

As I beetled past Dominic's I wondered if Kelly was awake yet. Probably not. As I remembered her she was good for another couple of hours. Only the heat would wake her. Then she would stretch that long lovely body, shower and dress in something cool and fetching. If I had time I would turn and wait for that to happen. But time was running out. For the murderer and me.

Near the courthouse I skidded into a parking place and went inside. Hulik's office clerk said he was out, didn't know when he'd be back. Didn't know where he was, either. Or wouldn't say.

I got back into the Volks. Sam Hulik was probably up on Crown Mountain poking through the ashes with the locals. Another death to sour his day. Nothing to do but wait for him to come back.

I chugged the Volks up the hill, parked and climbed slowly and unsteadily up the long flight of steps. They had never seemed steeper. At the top I paused, mopped my face and glanced over at the porch. Four people were sitting there. Not talking. Just staring at me: Allegra Tyner, Simon Hargrave, Kelly Martin and Sam Hulik.

I sidled toward them and said, "Where's Sonny?"

"Where the hell do you think he is?" Hulik growled. "Great defense attorney you are, Bentley. At least Meadows was around when he was wanted."

"Hard work never made up for talent." I strolled past them and inched behind the bar. With Norah gone everything was cafeteria style. I built a long fruity rum drink, loaded it with cubes and rested my back and elbows on the bar.

Hargrave growled, "You're taking all this damn coolly, Bentley."

"One man's opinion," I said. "Any more chatter from the peanut gallery?"

Hulik cleared his throat. He sounded mad. "Where were you last night?"

"Here and there," I said cheerfully. "Up hill and down dale to the sound of hunting horns. We'll get to all that, and in detail. It may even take a little time, so don't push me." I looked at Allegra. "When's Jamieson due?"

"Any time now, Steve. I sent Big John to meet him at the airport. The plane just landed."

"How's Sybil taking things?"

"Hard," Hulik said gruffly. "Now suppose you—"

I waggled one finger at him, drank from my glass and set it on the bar beside my left elbow. From my pocket I pulled Pierre's Colt and laid it beside the glass. I heard Kelly catch her breath.

"We are among thieves and murderers," I said. "When you need a roscoe you need it the most. There's no sending Johnny back to the closet to fetch it for you."

"Jesus Christ," Hargrave said disgustedly.

I waved my right hand. Hulik's face was stony. Kelly's held a trace of fear. I cleared my throat. "An active little island, Saint Thomas," I said moodily. "Peaceful as a riot in Cellhouse Nine and the murders average out to one a day." I ticked them off on my fingers: "Victor Polo, Reba Royce and Ralph Dominic."

"Wait a minute," Hulik interrupted. "We've identified what was left of Dominic's body by the bridgework. There's no evidence pointing to murder."

"No gun found?" I asked. "No garter thirty-two?"

"They're still sifting ashes."

Kelly shivered and turned away. Little Nemo had been hers.

I said, "It doesn't make a world of difference because the killer can only burn once. Take my word for it that Dominic was murdered. Sybil found him hidden out in the Crown Mountain house. I went there last night to bring him in but he was already dead. There was a length of garden hose looped over a rafter. Dominic's neck was in the noose at the other end. He was deader than Stalin."

"Why not suicide?" Hulik said surlily.

"A logical question, Sam. There wasn't a stool or a chair anywhere around he could have stepped from. Or jumped. And there was a buster mark on his forehead. He didn't sap himself, climb up on a chair, take the long drop and then get down and carry away the chair. He was sapped and hung there like a side of beef."

"By whom?" Hulik gritted.

"Nice use of the ablative. By someone big and strong enough to do it."

Kelly piped, "For God's sake, don't keep us cliffhanging."

"Never interrupt a man when he's got an audience. I'm tired and disillusioned. I've been sapped and dragged and busted, and last night I had to break out of a burning building to save my life. That's not fiction, beautiful. I've bullied old men and I've beat up younger ones until I'm sick of looking at pistol barrels. One more buster on the head and it'll pop like a water bag." I sipped my drink, gargled it a little and put the glass down again. "The story doesn't begin last night, friends, nor even the day Victor Polo came back here. It begins more than five years ago when Polo and Dominic were running the Casino as partners. Hell, maybe it begins the day Polo was born. But that's for social workers and tabloid writers to gnaw over." I looked down at my hand. It seemed far away. Remote. As though it belonged to someone else. I wondered if the fingers would still respond, if the index could still pull a trigger. I grunted and said, "In addition to running the Casino, Victor Polo had a sideline both interesting and profitable. *Victah Polo was a money mon. He make money any way he con.* Like the song says. And Victor Polo was a ponce."

"A what?" Hargrave bleated.

"A kind of pimp—a procurer, as the quality might say. He specialized in black ivory. Signed up colored girls for a nonexistent South American nightclub circuit. We'll assume he sampled the goods before shipment."

"Keep it clean," Kelly called.

"That's asking a lot, beautiful. Anyway, you get the picture: Polo working around the clock and not minding the effort at all. The girls never got back to the Islands, of course, so after a while word was whispered that Polo wasn't the most reliable booking agent in the Caribbean. I imagine it worried him less than a peeling nose. Now these girls weren't just served up from the sea on shells like Botticelli's Venus—they had families, relatives, even sweethearts. I can see one of the girls having a lover's tiff with her sweetheart and signing on with Polo. Maybe she told her sweetheart she'd come back in three or four months, but she never came. After a while that would set a man to pondering, even checking into what happened to other girls who went on Polo's tour. A little scratching around and you could make a pretty good case against Polo—the kind of case that's difficult to prove, but enough to make a man brood if he happened to love the girl. Who she was doesn't much matter because dead or alive she'll never be seen again. Let's brief the thing down to the abandoned lover working up a molten hate against Victor Polo and planning to do away with him the next moonless night. Only it doesn't work out that way."

I sipped enough to ease my throat, blinked and put aside the glass. Hooking my heel over the low rail, I stared up at the green parrot. It had its head under one wing, giving me the ignore treatment. I frowned and said, "He missed his chance because just then the Casino got hotter than a blowtorch and the owners had to split up and take off. Only at this point legend has it Dominic pulled the gypsy switch and Polo ended up aboard an open boat with a suitcase full of newspaper clippings, and a head filled with bitter memories. Dominic got all the loot. For one reason or another Polo didn't come back to Saint Thomas then—maybe he got word that Dominic couldn't be found and didn't know where else to look. In any case it's a matter of record that Polo got picked up in a Stateside bank heist and did a stretch in the big gray house, finally getting paroled a few months back. Now let's shift the focus back to Saint Thomas again. Things have cooled off or Dominic squared the rap and turns respectable or at least ostensibly so. With his take from the Casino he sets up his saloon and begins to take life easy, eventually marrying a girl as respectable as Sybil Drury. For Dominic it's a dull life, all sauce and no larceny. So he hires a Cha-Cha tough named Pierre Duroc and they start a contraband operation using the old Casino as a storehouse. Pierre lives handy by and when he's had a spat with his old woman there's an iron bed in the warehouse for him to pout on."

Kelly wrinkled her nose. "This is a free port, Steve. How on earth would—"

"Sure," I cut in, "but other islands aren't so liberal. Not the British Virgins nor the French islands. Luxury goods come here duty-free. What they're worth in Tortola and Anegada and Saint Martin represents a nice profit to a persevering smuggler. Pierre had a boat that could run stuff from Frenchtown to a lugger lying off Water Island. Not a big operation, just enough to nurse the glow of illegality in Dominic's crooked breast."

Allegra was craning her neck. I said, "We'll hear him when he comes. It shouldn't be long." A ball of ice was beginning to form in the pit of my stomach. My hand brushed the side of my face and the sweat was cold as grave water. I stretched my arms along the bar, rested more weight on them and went on. "That sets the scene for Polo's return. Dominic had gotten fat and sleek while Polo had pounded hard, hard rocks. From Kelly we know that Polo went to Vegas and lost what little green he had been able to save in stir. He flew down here intending to confront Dominic or rob him or beat the lost money out of him plus interest. Unluckily for Polo he was barely off the plane when he was recognized. And by the man who'd planned to take revenge on him five years before. That set the wheels in motion. The man—we'll call him the killer from now on—remembered Polo's predilection for coffee girls and shoved a decoy at him. None less than Reba Royce."

A gasp from Allegra. From a face white and strained.

"Yes, little Reba, beloved of many. She made a date with Polo and lured him down near the Casino that night for a bush shag."

Hargrave was staring at his thighs. His face was spotted with color. I said, "I can see Polo going there light of heart, glad to be back in familiar surroundings, perhaps even planning to sign up Reba for the long tour below the Equator. Anyway he goes there expecting everything except the knife the killer drives in his heart. They strip him and the killer wades out into the water with Polo's corpse and frees it to the tide. But next morning Pierre's father finds it drifting and tows it in. That was the first piece of bad luck for the killer. Polo's clothes, as we all know, were stashed in a trash can behind Reba's pad. A thoughtless slip-up but unimportant in the larger scheme."

"Why unimportant?" Hulik husked irritably.

"Because other errors were larger and more significant. Like Reba telling Dominic she'd been involved in Polo's disappearance. A likely boast from a woman to her lover, particularly when Dominic must have realized that Polo's return boded him little good."

"Can you prove any of that?" Hulik snapped.

"You'll get your witness." I turned my head and eyed the Colt. Even in repose it looked deadlier than a viper. "The killer now had a witness to his crime. What he needed was a way to dispose of Reba that would point to someone else, one of her lovers." I glanced at Hargrave. "He picked Sonny Tyner as the patsy for reasons we can all divine. The killer was a man who roamed a lot, who picked up whispers in the night. Either by chance or by astute planning he arranged Reba's death just after she'd had a public scene with Sonny. He took her down to the beach, stabbed her and hacked off her ring finger to give it the passion-crime touch. Through Norah Roberts he had the ring and the bag planted in Sonny's drawer—and found there by the same Norah. What hold he had over Norah the police will be able to find out. At this point Dominic decides to lie doggo. Maybe Dominic realized the killer knew Reba had mentioned the ambush to him; maybe he felt things were getting generally too hot. Anyway, with Pierre's aid he pulled the old Indian trick of walking into the water and emerging but leaving only one set of footprints. Pierre Duroc is available for those details. He'll have his arm in a cast for quite some time but he can still talk. Within this last hour he chattered like old Poll herself. To me."

"You intimidated him," Hulik accused.

"Such talk," I chided. "Let's say we reached an understanding. Pierre drew this gun on me and I took it away. In the process

Pierre got hurt. So we have Dominic hiding out in Reba's empty bungalow on Crown Mountain and the murderer knowing about it. Too bad for Dominic."

"How did he find out?" Hargrave asked.

"By watching, probably. By tailing Sybil, or by guessing. The killer knew about the Crown Mountain place, too. In its heyday I can see him as a frequent visitor." I let my glance drift over to Hargrave and settle there. "It must have been bad French comedy, lovers almost bumping into each other as they came and went, hiding behind screens and under the bed. Now—so long as Dominic lived he represented a menace to the killer's life. So Dominic had to die. And die he did. By the route already mentioned. When I was up there last night the killer came back, probably with a can of gasoline to get the blaze started, heard me walking around inside and waited for me. I never had a chance." Picking up the Colt, I slid a shell into the chamber and pushed the safety off.

Hulik called, "Hey, easy there."

"Guns are made to shoot," I said in a dead voice. "Last night I shot the killer. Only not with this gun. With a palm-size thirty-two that wasn't big enough." I stared down at Hargrave. "Feeling up to snuff today, Simon? All hale and hearty after a night with the tiger?"

Heavily he said, "You might have the decency to—"

"Crap," I spat. "Don't be a bible-parsing hypocrite. You've got your peace to make with Sonny and it's time you were figuring how to do it."

Allegra said, "Please. Steve, there's no need to be unpleasant."

I laughed nastily. "We're all too, too civilized, the lot of us. We've had murder and fornication and adultery thrown at us until the air stinks and all we do is mix iced drinks and chatter idly about the price of IBM. I'm sick of it. I want truth. I want it in big fresh bucketfuls, sloshing the scuppers clean." I gripped the Colt and stared at them. A nerve twitched in my face.

Just then I heard the sound of an engine climbing the hill. It strained upward, coughed and died at the foot of the steps. A car door opened, Allegra stood up. She smiled nervously and said, "That must be Mr. Jamieson."

"Have him come right up," I said. "I wouldn't want him to miss the finale for lollipops."

Kelly got up and came over to me. I said, "Stand away, beautiful, there's still some facts to be told." Her shoulders seemed to slump. Turning, she went back to her seat.

Footsteps ascending. Finally the top of his head. His steel-gray hair was short and combed forward like a Princeton senior. He was a little shorter than I was and he had a handsome face and a cheerful grin. He wore a white linen suit, open collar shirt and his right hand carried a pigskin attaché case. Tremayne Jamieson, Esquire, of Number One Wall Street. Everyone stared at him.

I was staring beyond him. Up the stairway came a curly black head and a set of teeth whiter than piano keys. Big John, the cabbie. As Allegra went forward to greet Jamieson, I moved away from the bar. Big John came onto the veranda carrying Jamieson's suitcase, one of those lightweight aluminum weekenders covered with beige fabric. Big John set it down and turned to go. With my left hand I pulled a five-dollar bill from my pocket and called, "Hey, I owe you something from the other day."

Big John turned and stared at me. He should have said something but he didn't. His mouth opened and then it closed. His eyes got bigger. I said, "You remember me, Big John. The airport the other day? Mr. Bentley? Mr. Tyner's friend?"

His arms were as long as gallows. The hands opened and closed. From the shoulders down he began to shake.

The veranda was as silent as Mammoth Cave. I said, "Speak up, Big John. Unless you think I'm a ghost."

His legs were shivering, his shoes rattled the flooring. I said, "You remember me, but not from the airport alone. You remember me from last night. Up on Crown Mountain. When you slugged me and burned Reba's house."

A sigh went around the circle behind me. I listened to it instead of watching him. And when he moved it was like a snake striking. One hand flicked into a pocket and I saw the flash of metal. My Colt was halfway up and a shot barked out, then a second almost fusing with the first. I had thrown myself back against the bar but I was too late. The big black man was sinking to his knees, both arms clutching his belly. His chin was slumped against his chest and I could hear blood burbling in his throat. From beside me someone moved, a big blond man with a smoking revolver in his hand, a blued .38 Detective Special, easy on the draw and ample for the heavy work. A specimen of the work sank closer to the flooring, teetered sideways and collapsed. When I reached him his eyes were starred with the cataracts of death.

From behind me nervous female sobbing. In a corner of the veranda stood Tremayne Jamieson, stiller than a lead statue. The fingers around the grip of his attaché case were whiter than sanded bone. I knelt beside the big dead bulk and ripped open the damp shirt. Closer than the span of a hand two holes punctured the thorax, stabbed by two steely fingers. In each one glistened an ooze of bright blood. Plastered across the left rib, high and near the armpit, was a crude bandage stained with dried blood. "There's your killer," I said in a cracked voice. "Court adjourned."

CHAPTER SEVENTEEN

Another day. The sky was light azure and filmy cirrus clouds floated higher than a maiden's hopes. By the wet bulb hygrometer the humidity was something under twenty per cent and in the sunlight the mercury poked just over ninety-three.

In the shade where I was sitting the temperature was twenty degrees kinder, but under my bandages the skin felt as though red ants were holding a jamboree. My noggin was only dented, not fissured, and most of the pain had gone away. That or I was getting used to it.

The white-capped nurse came down the stairs and onto the veranda. Her overnight bag was in one hand and her black dressing bag in the other. Severely she said, "Just because I'm leaving doesn't mean you're fit to do calisthenics, Mr. Bentley."

"No, ma'am."

"And don't remove the bandages until tomorrow. If you shouldn't want to come to the clinic use carbon tet. That way you wouldn't lose any more hair."

"Thank you, ma'am."

From his hassock Sonny said, "Send me the bill, Gertrude."

"Yes, sir. Have a good trip, you and Mrs. Tyner." She fussed with her cape, got a no-nonsense grip on the overnight bag and began walking down the Stone steps.

My left arm was stiff but not so stiff I couldn't boost a cigarette. When I had it going, I said, "How long a holiday?"

"Two months, anyway, Maybe more. The children will join us in Paris. From there we'll head for the Bernese Oberland and play it by ear. Hell, maybe we'll stay on for the winter season. I haven't skied at Chamonix since I was a kid."

"Me neither. Much less Garmisch and Innsbruck."

Sonny glanced at me and laughed self-consciously. "Always the deft needle."

"Coming back here?"

"I'm not sure. What are your plans?"

I let smoke drift upward to where the parrot was sleeping upside down. "There's maybe a day's work left on Coco Isle. I'll get around to it tomorrow. After that it'll be back to the District of Columbia. And positively no more excitement until next Saint Patrick's Day."

"Need Simon's signature on anything else?"

"Nothing I can think of. Why?"

"He pulled out of here earlier this morning."

"Headed where?"

"Florida." He coughed and looked away. He seemed to be studying a crack in the paint. I couldn't see it.

"What else?"

"Well, Sybil flew there, too. On a different plane."

"Sounds like connivance."

"In a way. They're going to be married."

"June and January," I mused. "Well, let's hope the experience does them some good. At the least it'll be a change."

"It'll be all of that," he said wistfully. "Oh, your check's in an envelope in the office."

"Thanks. But that isn't all you owe me."

"I know. A great deal of gratitude."

"Stuff. I mean greenbacks. Ninety of them."

"Do I? For what?"

"Blood money. Plus four hundred and ten to old Henry Royce. He's earned it a few times over."

"Mmm. Why don't I just give you the whole five hundred and you pay him?"

"We could do that," I said, "but there's human values to consider. For instance I want you to meet Reba's father."

"I see," he said thoughtfully. "I'm not getting off as lightly as I thought."

"No. You'll find him pegged out over in Frenchtown. His favorite tree is just outside the bar."

He took a deep breath. "I'll take care of it." Peeling some bills from a roll he got up and brought them over. I shoveled them in my pocket. My ninety-buck investment back.

"Our plane leaves at five, Steve. You're still pretty rocky so we won't expect you among the delegation."

"I'd be only a wraith in the crowd."

"Well," he said and stuck out his hand, "I should be helping Allegra pack. Lawyer Meadows will be around later. He'll be manager while we're gone."

"He'll love having me here," I said and shook his hand. "Me and the parrot." Then he turned and went up the stairs, his sponge soles making less noise than the bellow of a bull minnow. I sat where I was, smoking and thinking until the cigarette warmed my fingers and I stubbed it out and got up. My legs were rubbery from nearly two days in bed, sedatives and a generally rundown constitution. I wobbled over to the bar and built a drink. No more Cruzan shinny. What I was pouring into my glass had been shipped from the Firth of Forth. I savored its bouquet, plopped in an ice cube and sat down again.

Yesterday morning Kelly had stopped at my bedside long enough to say she and Tremayne were outward bound for a day's sail around the island. Today was more of the same. Too bad I couldn't have come along. Lifting my glass, I gazed at the amber fluid. "Liar," a voice said. Along the empty veranda it had a melancholy ring. I fed myself another cigarette, leaned back and stared up at the overhead. The parrot was untangling himself and twitching his tail feathers. After a while he would amble down and climb the cocktail table for the usual handouts. "Easy times are past, Jack," I murmured. "Have to work for it now like everyone else."

I frowned. All this talking to myself was too much like an early O'Neill play—the one with the crazy masks. It was time to change the scene. Like the parrot I had better get to work.

I got down most of my drink and then I got up and put on my sun glasses. From the top of the stairway I could see a white cruise ship making for the West India dock, rigging a-flutter with frivolous pennants. In a little while its gangplank would disgorge another troupe of feather merchants to plunder gift shoppes and gladden Island hearts.

With a lot of help from the iron railing I managed to make it all the way to the road without getting the fantods. The Volks was no hotter than a hundred and twenty inside and the steering wheel was incandescent. Favoring the Gold Coast custom of taking your parasol everywhere, I guided my motorized chair down to the square and squeezed it into a meter of palm-tree shade. Then I got out and pushed the swinging doors into the old coal mine.

The boar's nest hadn't changed much. It was one of those places where the background never changes. The same frayed blond barkeep with the same varnished smile, the same too-chatty waitresses and the same heavily busted Indian bimbo squatting on the same cushioned too-small stool. Anyone seeking a clean, well-lighted place apply elsewhere. I wondered if she told fortunes in her off-hours—if she had any. Drinking and rolling dice could keep a bosco plenty occupied if she put her mind to it. And this one did. Except now her lazy almond eyes were watching me cross the floor. I was supposed to take notice and begin purring hungrily. Only that took more energy than I was willing to muster. I had barely enough to make it to my favorite table and slump into the same uncomfortable chair. Her sensual lips took on a slight frown. Either she was losing her appeal or I was a male who needed glasses badly. I let her gnaw on it with no help from me. The waitress with the beach squint took my order and sailed back with my scotch in less time than it takes to count to a thousand by twos.

Overhead the blades of a big propeller fan stirred the cool air. Casaba Chest had given me up as myopic and was sharing a dirty joke with the blond barkeep. It looked like a great life. In an hour or so the place would be jammed with cheerful boosters from Akron and general high jinks would begin.

I dipped a finger into the glass and poked at the single ice cube. The swinging doors opened and a woman came in. Not a lithe young thing in trim pantaloons and wedgies but a slumped old woman in a flour-sack dress. She peered into the gloom, blinked a few times and headed for me. When she reached the table she wrenched out the other chair and plumped herself down. "Hi, Ma," I said. "Have a drink."

Vane Drury said, "You heard about Sybil—and Simon ?"

"News travels."

"That all you have to say?" she snapped.

I lifted my glass. "We could toast a couple of four-flushers—but maybe you wouldn't like it."

"I don't—particularly. You're usually pretty lively with your tongue, young man. No other thoughts?"

"One," I said. "Disreputable, but a thought, nevertheless."

"Go ahead."

"As a famous diva once said: 'Thank God for the peace and tranquillity of the nuptial couch, after the hurly-burly of the chaise-longue.'"

She was chewing her lower lip. A trifle untidily. After a while she said, "I guess I get it. It'll be strange having Simon for a son-in-law. The whole thing's ridiculous. He's much too old for Sybil."

"Why not let her take her own lumps this time? I'll bet she didn't marry Dominic half as much to get him as to get away from you. And I'll say this, too: you're every inch a man."

She glared at me. "That's a hateful thing to say."

I shrugged. "Basically I'm a coarse fellow. All the same, think it over."

She sucked in a deep breath, our glances locked and she said fiercely, "Well, where's that drink you mentioned?"

It came in due course, we toasted the newlyweds and then she got up and waddled over to the bar. The Indian produced a leather dice cup, made a few trial rolls and the game was on. I paid my score, got up and sidled out. Nobody noticed me leaving. Least of all the blonde with the varnished smile. Her eyes were fixed on the moving dice cup and they were harder than Mexican agates.

Parked across from the courthouse was a trailer dog wagon on axle blocks. I navigated to it and ordered a double hamburger with onions and relish and a pint of milk. From the curb a little colored kid watched me wistfully. I motioned him over and bought him a chocolate milkshake. He sucked it up so fast the straws bulged. Pressing a quarter in his palm, I said, "You can do a small favor for me."

"Sure, mon."

"Go up the courthouse steps and yell for Mister Hulik. He'll be a big man, as tall as a mast and wider than the doorway. Holler someone's sticking up the dog wagon. Tell him to hurry."

His eyes danced with deviltry. "That all?"

"It'll do."

Grinning, he skipped away and scooted up the steps. I finished my pint of moo, sanded my lips on a paper napkin and paid the girl. When I turned around Sam Hulik was running down the steps. He made me and slowed. Shrugging, he came over.

I said, "Ever rain around here?"

"Some. Forty inches a year."

"Just a morning mist in Manaos. You bolt pretty good—for a fellow dedicated to a sedentary life. What's it like to be a hero?"

"As if you didn't know."

I squinted up at the sky. "There's several bars I haven't visited yet. Call it quits for the day and let's do a little serious guzzling."

A smile flickered over his face. "Wish I could, Steve. You know the rules."

"Hell, you deserve some fun. It's been two whole days since you killed anyone."

"Yeah," he said. "There's that." He forked an elbow against the side of the dog wagon and scratched the side of his face. "While we're on the subject, how long ago did you start to figure Big John as the killer?"

"Late in the game," I admitted. "Almost too late. Norah turning up the ring and bag made it too damn pat. Maybe you saw that, too."

He nodded. "We picked up Tyner because that was what we were supposed to do. But I was far from convinced he was the killer. I figured we'd play along and see if the killer relaxed, made a slip. Only there weren't any slips and Dominic got killed."

"Norah wasn't very bright," I said. "I had Kelly follow her that night. She went straight down the street to Big John's cab booth. Once I began to think of him as a possibility the knifings seemed natural. And I remembered seeing him slap old Henry around over at the Normandie. It wasn't much but it seemed enough out of character to set me wondering. And it took a man with a lot of muscle to heave Dominic's dead weight up into that noose." I felt myself shiver a little. Even in the sunlight.

Hulik said, "In case you wondered why Norah would do what she did for Big John, there's an answer. And not a pretty one. Seven years ago Norah signed up with Polo for the long trip South. Last year she made it back—what was left of her, anyway. In killing Polo, Big John wiped out a lot of her pain and suffering. So she helped him. Not for money or love, not even because she had anything against Mr. Tyner. But to help a man who had done her a favor." He glanced at his wristwatch. "I'm flying back to San Juan in an hour. Guess you'll be gone when I pass through again." He stuck out a big hand. It covered mine with enough to spare for two flapjacks. "We'll have that drink one day. And it'll be my pleasure."

Then he turned and walked back to the courthouse.

Beside me my small conspirator materialized. "I do it right?"

"You did it perfect." I flipped another quarter at him and went back to the Volks and crawled inside. The seat was bearably warm and the steering wheel had cooled some. Between the drinks and high tea at the dog wagon I was feeling a lot more like someone I remembered instead of the groggy stranger with a gimp shoulder and clown bandages. Starting the engine, I made for the waterfront and as I beetled along I saw the *Seabiscuit* moored alongside the pier. Rip Andersen was standing on the poop supervising a working party. Stores were being loaded. Enough champagne was going aboard to float a minesweeper. Slowly I steered alongside and stopped. Andersen squinted at me and waved. Then he jumped to the pier and came over. I said, "Contrabanding, or is all that bubbly for on-board consumption?"

"Right," he said. "I got myself a charter. Dough in advance this time."

"Congrats. Anybody I know?"

He stared down at something on the pier and kicked at it. I didn't see what it was. Maybe it wasn't anything at all. "Could be," he said, and looked up. "Funny. I sort of thought you might know."

I felt my belly tighten. My lips went stiff. "I've been feeling poorly lately," I said. "I guess someone just neglected to bring me the news."

"It's for tomorrow," he said quietly. "First port of call Palm Beach. Then up the Inland Waterway to Connecticut. Westport, to be exact."

I wet parched lips. "That makes her as exclusive as the YMCA."

"You know better than that, Steve."

"Yeah," I said. "I guess I do." Then I slid the car into gear and pulled ahead. I let it idle along the promenade a block or so and then I turned into Dominic's and parked beside the same scrawny shade tree. I got out slowly, walked around back and climbed up the stairway to the hall. It was shadowy there and a light dry breeze drifted along the hall. Maybe it had pushed her door a jar or maybe she had just left it that way. From where I stood I could see inside a dark room. One white bag was already packed. The other lay open across the seat of a chair, partly filled with filmy trifles. The breeze ruffled them, I swallowed and went in.

She was lying on the bed, face down, her face turned away from the door and slanted into the pillow. Her hair was tousled as though fingers had worried it a good long time. The room was quiet enough that I could hear her breathing. Not the shallow regular breathing of sleep but heavier and uneven. A muffled voice said, "Steve?"

"Who else? Borrow a case of sherry?"

Her face turned and her lips moved. "How are you fee—"

"Great," I said. "Two more vitamin pills and I can wade in and clean up the zoo. Panther pen and all."

Below her eyes lay patches that clung like air-brushed silver. A small handkerchief dried them and she looked up at me. Her voice was one decibel above a whisper. "Steve—I—I've got something to tell you."

"Hell," I said gruffly, "the whole town knows. And they say Palm Beach is a good town to pick up an offseason trousseau."

"Do they? That's nice of them. What do you say, darling?"

I was feeling unsteady enough to sit down in the chair beside her bed. Between my hands hers was cool and damp. "You don't owe me a thing, Irish. All you ever did was lend me Little Nemo—and I lost that for you."

She laughed tautly. "He says he loves me, Steve. I hope he does."

"What about you?"

"I want to love him, too."

I patted her hand. "Then you probably will. Just don't give up trying."

"I don't suppose you'd be willing to kiss the bride?"

"I would," I said, "if she happened to be mine." But I bent over anyway and kissed the side of her neck, high up and near her ivory ear. I felt a quiver go through her body and then she said quietly, "You know all about everything, darling. He's different. There's a lot his world doesn't know about—things I'll never tell him. You're different. You know me through and through. Once I might have been right for you—too long ago. But not since then. Not ever."

I lifted her hand and let my lips linger on the back of it. The skin was smoother than smooth velvet. "You're a lot of different people, Irish. You're little Jean O'Houlihan and the starlet on the casting couch; the rich man's snooty mistress and a girl who hikes back from a petting party. It's time to choose a character for keeps."

"I will," she whispered. "Believe me."

I stood up then and walked away from her. Swallowing hard, I walked down the hall to the steps and out into the sunlight. I plodded over the sand to the Volks and then I got behind the wheel. Sunlight had made my eyes smart. I got out my handkerchief and blew my nose. Then I started the engine and backed around and drove across to the waterfront promenade.

The wind had freshened and out in the bay an old battered lugger was standing out for Tortola, patched canvas spanking in the quartering breeze. I watched until its sails were no larger than the wings of a gull and then I drove back to town.

THE END

www.ingramcontent.com/pod-product-compliance
Lightning Source LLC
Chambersburg PA
CBHW030343180626
46812CB00007B/2739